Child of the Lots

Child of the Lots

by

Winnie Walsh

DORRANCE PUBLISHING CO., INC.
PITTSBURGH, PENNSYLVANIA 15222

All Rights Reserved
Copyright © 2004 by Winnie Walsh
No part of this book may be reproduced or transmitted
in any form or by any means, electronic or mechanical,
including photocopying, recording, or by any information
storage and retrieval system without permission in
writing from the publisher.

ISBN # 0-8059-6518-1
Printed in the United States of America

First Printing

For information or to order additional books, please write:
Dorrance Publishing Co., Inc.
701 Smithfield Street
Third Floor
Pittsburgh, Pennsylvania 15222
U.S.A.
1-800-788-7654
Or visit our web site and on-line catalog at www.dorrancepublishing.com

To my children and grandchildren.

Acknowledgments

I wish to thank Bianca Stewart, whose belief in me encouraged the writing of *Child of the Lots*. My appreciation to Rosemary Daniell and her Zona Rosa workshops for their help to me to stay focused and never give up.

Special thanks to the Bronx Historical Society for their research.

Prologue

Webster defines lot; n., one of a set of objects drawn when making a decision by chance; the use of these objects for selection; a person's fortune in life; the site for making movies; a number of person or things considered as a group or unit.

To many South Bronx children the lots on Intervale Avenue were all of the above.

Summer or winter, activities abounded. In the heat of summer, one passing the city-long block of Pompeii-type ruins could see children of all ages, colors, size, and shape darting back and forth in games of tag, hide and seek, jumping canyons of spaces between broken walls and concrete. In the late 1930s and early 1940s organized children's play was unheard of, at least in that part of the world.

In winter one could find the children huddled around huge bonfires, while an older boy who usually took charge of the ritual of roasting mickies handed them out to the group. Small children's fingers peeking through cut-off woolen gloves would flip the potato back and forth, cooling it in the process. Once the black burnt skin was removed, little was left to wolf down, but the excitement and camaraderie shared by the children made up for the small portions. These scenes would be witnessed around dusk after a day of sledding on the one sloping mountain. Discarded flat cartons that were used earlier in the day as sleds served as kindling to start the fire going. The potatoes came from some unsuspecting Irish household.

Chapter One

"Sit down," Patrick said. Mr. And Mrs. McSweeney filed into the small kitchen. Mrs. McSweeney's beady eyes scanned the worn gray chrome kitchen chairs to see which one had the most padding to support her enormous frame comfortably. The McSweeneys lived on Kelley Street in the South Bronx just around the corner from the O'Connors. Hugh McSweeney and Patrick O'Connor lived in Donegal, Ireland, as children on neighboring farms, and upon migrating to the Untied States in the late 1920s they remained friends. They both had attended The Delehanty Institute in Manhattan and managed to acquire stationary engineers licenses between drinking bouts.

"Will you be taking a cup of tea?" asked Mrs. O'Connor.

"Oh, don't be going' to any trouble, Bridget. How's Conrad anyway?" McSweeney asked, settling in a chair and lighting up his pipe. Bridget reached up for the canister of tea in the cupboard.

"We'll try tea bags for a change," she said; "loose tea has gotten scarce. People seem to say these are just as good. I don't think so, but we'll give it a go. I had a letter last week. It takes a long time for a letter to come, but Ellen said he was getting on. He came home from the hospital after a day or so."

"Sure there's not much wrong with him," blurted Patrick, "big strapping guy like Con. It'd take a might to knock him off his pins."

"Aye, to be sure," Paddy McSweeney said, giving his pipe another light. "But he must have been given a good scare."

Unlike the O'Connors and McSweeneys migrating to the States, Conrad Breslin, Bridget's brother, decided to go to Sydney, Australia, and settle. Upon doing so he had met and married Ellen. Ellen's family had a clock business, and while Conrad apprenticed at the shop, their romance started. Upon the death of Ellen's parents, Ellen, being the only child, inherited the thriving store. They had no children, and with the birth of their niece Una and nephew Tim, their lack of family quickly involved them in corresponding regularly as to the development of their Yankee relatives. Letters and packages from Australia were constantly coming and going, and when the children started school they too wrote regularly.

"Did they ever find out what caused the pains in his chest?"

"His heart; rest is what he needs, the doctor said. He's to rest for a few weeks." Bridget turned to the whistling teakettle, picked it up, rinsed the porcelain teapot with the hot water, and then dropped four tea bags into it. "There, we'll let it steep awhile and then give it a go."

"Away you go, cat," Mrs. McSweeney said, pushing the cat away form her leg and nearly falling off the chair. "You'll run my stockings," she chided the cat. "Is that thing having another litter?"

"Aye, she is," said Bridget. "Want some Annie?" she smiled.

"Indeed I do not," pouted Mrs. McSweeney, indignant at the offer. "I have enough to feed without a cat about. Why don't you drown it?"

"Musha, don't you know you're not home, Annie?" they have the SPCA here. You could go to jail for doing something like that. Besides, I don't think I could do away with her; she's no bother to me."

"Ah Bridget, you've gone daft since you've been in the States." Mrs. McSweeney said, waving her hand to emphasize her point.

"The tea's ready for pouring; sit into the table Hugh. Padric, give me the other chair round here." Bridget motioned with her hand and the group drank tea and ate soda bread, which was cut into serving pieces. When the tea was over, McSweeney asked Patrick to play a few tunes on his fiddle. Bridget hoped her husband would decline because the fiddle playing usually lasted an hour or two, and after the men had a few drinks she knew her husband would invite them to stay for dinner.

"Would you like a tune, Hugh?" smiled Patrick.

"Indeed it would hit the spot," McSweeney said, putting the pipe down and settling back in his chair. Patrick got the fiddle out, and the group moved to the porch just in back of the kitchen.

Bridget stayed behind muttering to herself, "Now what will I ever do about dinner?"

"Are you coming out, Bridget?" Annie poked her head back in through the open door.

"Yes, I'll be right there. I want to see to the tea things," Bridget hollered back.

"Oh, leave them," said her husband. "You can do that again. And so she took off her apron and joined the group. After an hour or so the men were feeling their drinks, and her husband invited them to dinner. Bridget went in and started looking for cans of soup and Spam to stretch out a dinner that she had hoped would be for herself, Una, and her husband. But the small chicken would never feed five adults, and she angrily pushed the cans back and forth in the cupboard.

"Why don't they ever go home? No manners I say," Bridget muttered as she stacked the dishes in the kitchen sink and reset the table for dinner.

"I'm home, Mom." The front door slammed shut, and Una hollered from the hallway, "Something smells good." She sailed into the kitchen, brushing in back of her mother, sniffing and raising a lid from a pot on the stove. Her mother made a silent motion with her head toward the back porch. "Oh no," Una whispered, "are the McSweeneys here again? Why don't they just move in with us?"

"Shush, don't be so fresh, and mind your manners," her mother scolded.

"I bet they're both sloshed," Una said disgustedly. "I'm not hungry. I'll eat later after they go home. I'm not in the mood for stories about the old country or when am I going to settle down."

"Suit yourself; I'll keep a plate hot for you and you can eat it later."

"Thanks Mom." Una walked back down the short hall and into her room. The mirror that hung over her dresser held souvenirs of places she and Andrew had been. The menu from the Lido was pasted on one corner. Chopsticks from the Chinese restaurant on Southern Boulevard were tied together with pink ribbon and hung askew on either side of the frame. She stared at herself in the mirror and turned sideways. *It just can't be*, she said to herself. *Oh God, it just can't be. We only did it once. That one time in City Island.* She remembered how Andrew had always wanted to go all the way, but she held firm and strong until that night: the candlelight dinner at the Lido, the dancing to all that dreamy music. She didn't normally drink that much, but Andrew said the champagne would be wasted if they didn't finish the magnum. The mood of lovemaking had spilled over into the back seat of his car that particular night because Andrew had set the stage perfectly.

It had been only four weeks ago, Memorial Day weekend, but her period was one week late and she was upset. Andrew never mentioned Jean's name that night, and Una just took it for granted that he didn't want to spoil the romantic mood by bringing up an old argument. Since then, the few times she had seen Andrew she felt uncomfortable around him and sensed something was wrong. His phone calls, which used to be nightly, became sporadic. When he did call, his voice seemed troubled and pretentious. There was definitely something very wrong.

The short heavy-set priest waddled over to the pulpit, ascended the stairs, and motioned to the altar boy to turn off the oscillating fan just below him. His monotonous voice replaced the drone of the whirring fan. Members of the congregation substituted hymnals for fans, seeking some relief from the oppressive heat. Two infants were fussing in the pew Una occupied, and when the priest raised his voice to intone the announcements they became rigid in their mother's arms.

"And the banns of matrimony are announced for the first time between Andrew Mulligan and Jean Mahoney." Una's eyes filled with tears. She removed her sunglasses, blotted her eyes with a tissue, and waited for the collection, which she thought would never come. The priest's voice lowered and continued in its boring tone. Finally, the ushers started up the aisles of the church, and as soon as they did Una stood up in the pew and climbed past the knees of people. She headed for the exit, bolted down the church steps, and started home. Beads of perspiration dripped from her hairline. Tears mingled with sweat produced a salty taste in her mouth. She half ran and half walked the eight blocks to her house. The dark hallway allowed very little light, and she had to feel for the opening in the lock of the door to insert the key because by now she was sobbing uncontrollably.

She flung open her bedroom door and dashed over to her dresser. Her hands reached up wildly and ripped off all the mementos that adorned her vanity. In a frenzy, she tore the menus and snapped the chopsticks in two. "How could he?" she wailed over and over. She screamed a question that had no answer. "How could I have been so stupid?"

In her mind she saw the Andrew of a year before. Couldn't she see through those lying blue eyes of his as he convincingly revealed the soap opera of the century? His baseball career had exploded into the minor leagues right after high school. Offers had come from the Yankees and Dodgers. People he thought never liked him suddenly became his friends. Invitations to parties abounded when he came home from the Yankee farm team after each season. And then his world caved in on him. He had contracted yellow jaundice. The invitations stopped as quickly as his contract with the Yankees did. Friends disappeared—all but one: Jean Mahoney. She visited him faithfully, and he believed he owed her something and that something was an engagement ring.

"How stupid could I have been?" she cried and hit her pillow as if she were smashing him with her fists. Exhausted, she fell off to sleep.

"Anybody home?" Una heard her mother's voice and stared up at the ceiling. "It's awfully hot in here, Padric; open the window in the living room and let some air in." Again her mother's voice, "Una," and a knock on her door. "Oh, you are home. What are you doing in bed this time of day? What's wrong? What is it? You've been crying, darlin'. You look awful."

"Oh Ma, it's just awful," she sobbed. "He's getting married."

"Who's getting married?" Her mother frowned.

"Andrew," Una whispered.

"I knew it," her mother said, turning her face away from her daughter to open the window in the bedroom. "Now, now," she forced herself to control her anger and walked toward the bed and gently picked Una up in her arms, caressing her head, patting her hair, rocking her back and forth. "There's no sense me telling you I told you so when I found out about the other girl: shush there, there now." She kept rocking. "You're too good for him anyway. If he's busy two-timing women now, imagine what he'd be like after the wedding. It's probably all for the best. Shh, there, there now come outside on the porch and have some iced tea."

Una heaved sobs and buried her head on her mothers' shoulders. "How could he lie like that? He told me he loved me, Ma, not her."

"How did you find out?" her mother asked, gently pushing her back.

"In church this morning. It was announced from the pulpit," Una said, crying between every few words.

"Better to have found out before than later. If he did carry on with you while he was engaged, I don't think he'll be any different when he's married. You're better off, and good riddance I say."

"Oh Mom you don't know how I feel. You just know he lied; everything was a lie, everything." She went back to sobbing.

"What's goin' on in here? Is she sick?" Her father poked his head in the doorway.

"No," said his wife, "she's been disappointed by the boyfriend. She'll be all right."

"Is that the reason for all this ruckus? Sure there's plenty of fish in the sea. Don't be worrying yourself, darlin. It's his loss. There's someone just around the bend for you, don't be breaking your heart." Her father turned and left.

"Oh, Mom, how could he?"

"I don't know, but you can be sure his girlfriend must have found out about you and put the question to him and decided he had to, and as your father said, it's his loss. Don't be breakin' your heart." Her mother rose from the bed and Una turned her body toward the wall, still weeping. "Come on, now have some iced tea, wash your face, and come out to the porch; it's so much cooler out there."

"I don't feel like it, Ma, not now, maybe in a while."

Chapter Two

Una stood dangerously close to the edge of the subway platform peering down the tracks. The train whizzed by, creating a cyclone effect on her freshly pressed cotton skirt. Her hands smoothed the billowing material while her head darted back and forth, trying to judge where the third car from the end would stop. Somehow her friend Marta Perusi, who rode to work every day with her managed to save her a seat. Ever since graduation from Cathedral High School they kept in touch. Marta lived across the street from the Simpson Street police station, and she was never short on dates. Many times Marta tried to convince Una to go on a blind date with one of the policeman, but Una always refused.

Marta's parents were Italian and very strict about dating. Many times she used Una as a ploy in her love life. Marta's father and mother had thick Italian accents, and whenever a prospective date showed up they both grilled the unsuspecting young man relentlessly, so Marta adopted her own date policymaking. Making arrangements to meet her escort in places other than her home, when she knew the date would entail an affair that might last until after midnight, she told her parents she would be sleeping at Una's house.

Sometimes Marta told situations that ended up with the two girls laughing hysterically. Like the time a police officer with the name Joseph Botts came courting. After the initial introduction, Mr. Perusi kept calling him Dufus, and to make matters worse his wife would chime in occasionally and call him Dufus as well. Needless to say Joseph Botts never came calling again because even though the girls could laugh at the situation, Marta didn't appreciate him telling the company that shared the double date that particular night about her parents' thick Italian accents.

Screeching brakes brought the train to a halt. The subway doors opened and the people standing on the subway platform scrambled through, pushing and shoving, bumping each other, eyeing empty seats, and dashing to occupy them.

"Over here." Una turned in the direction of the shrill voice. "Over here Una," Marta shrieked again. Una spun around the pole and caught Marta practically lying across the empty seat she had saved from the thundering herd of humanity swarming down the aisle.

Una pushed her way through the sea of bodies. "Thanks, Mart, what a lucky break to get a seat," she said as she positioned herself next to Marta's thin, model-like body. Marta's dark hair framed a face that strongly resembled Ava Gardner, the popular Hollywood movie actress. She had high cheekbones and dark brown eyes with thick black lashes that she extended with mascara and which sometimes left dark circles under her eyes.

"What's the matter?" Marta knew her friend too long not to notice that Una was unusually quiet.

"Oh, Mart, he's getting married…he's marrying Jean," Una lamented.

"No! He's not," Marta's voice caught the ears of nosy straphangers. "Not after what you told me about the night in City Island." Una had shared her happiness of that night over a month ago with her best friend, and the two of them believed they would be shopping for bridal attire very soon.

"And that's not the worst of it." Una crimped her hand over her mouth and whispered in her friend's ear, "I'm pregnant. I'm late and I'm sure I'm pregnant."

"Oh my God, what will you do? You'll have to tell him; after all it's his baby." Taking Una's lead, Marta lowered her voice.

"Oh, Mart, I can't. I don't want him now after all those lies. He was just using me, that's all, he never had any intention of marrying me," Una lamented.

"Una, you've got to tell him; what will you do?"

"I haven't decided yet."

"Have you told your mom yet?"

"No, not until I have some sort of plan. She will be terribly hurt and my father will probably want to shoot him. That's something I'm not looking forward to." The train took on new passengers and the two girls continued discussing Una's dilemma.

"Maybe you could put an ad in the paper. I read about a girl one time who got in the family way and a couple adopted the baby," said Marta.

"That's not a bad idea, Mart. I could put a personal ad in *The New York Times*."

"Oh, there's my stop," Marta jumped up and started pushing through the crowd. Turning her head she yelled, "Don't worry, we'll figure out something. Una managed a faint smile as Marta disappeared. Marta's seat filled quickly with the pivot of a male strap hanger sending whiffs of his after shave lotion in Una's direction. *Men*—the word vibrated in Una's thoughts as she shot a look of annoyance at the unsuspecting rider.

The rush of cool air in the lobby of 35 Wall Street welcomed the bustling throng spinning through the revolving doors of the skyscraper. Comments about relief from the heat filled the conversations of the people heading for the elevators. Una felt her own body temperature drop as she listened to the crowd of people muttering to one another while milling around the elevator doors.

"Hello there," a voice behind Una said. She turned around and recognized Mr. Nightingale. His voice matched his name. Mr. Nightingale headed the corporate syndicate department in Una's firm. With his soft-spoken voice, she often wondered how he managed to aspire to such a demanding job. But his department ran smoothly and there never seemed to be any gossiping or backbiting. He treated the young women of the office in the most courteous way, unlike some of the salesmen or the guys who worked in the bond cages, who flirted constantly. When Una decided to take night courses at Fordham University, he had inquired regularly how school was going, and at Christmas parties he acted more like a father than a boss, protecting the young girls from the passes of some men who had imbibed too much.

An elevator door opened and she, along with Mr. Nightingale, hustled into the empty cage. They stood side by side now. "A welcome relief to come to work today," he said, smiling.

"Yes, although I think the beach would top that."

"For you maybe, not me. I would burn to a crisp. I'll settle for an air-conditioned building."

Una remained silent, *Sure, you're the boss; you can sit and spread the newspaper out on your desk and read all morning even though we have four bids scheduled for eleven o'clock. And if we win all four I'll be working till midnight getting out confirmations.*

"Are you all right?" he asked, noting her preoccupation.

"I'm just thinking about our busy schedule today and that the beach is the place I would rather be." She felt guilty about the lie. Of all the men in the office he deserved an honest answer and she should have ended the remark with the "busy schedule today." On the twenty-second floor they went their separate ways.

At eleven o'clock, four bids caused a constant stream of blazing lights on the trading board. The desk blazed constantly. No sooner had one call been answered when another bulb pulsed bright again. Salesmen never heeded the rule of not coming into the trading desk room during bid time even though the firm had moved the municipal traders' desk into a glass-enclosed private office with chalkboards. During bidding time it became impossible to hear on the phone with salesmen hovering over the traders' shoulders. The salesmen flocked like locusts around the desk, making it difficult for the traders to hear on the phones. Salesmen were supposed to stay outside and peer through the window to read the result of the bids, but they never did, especially if the firm was winning the bid from a competing syndicate. *Good*, she thought to herself, *we lost that one.*

She quickly pushed in to answer another call. "Una, it's Andrew." One of the salesmen hovered over her pressing her for information on another bid.

"Mr. Rudman," Una turned, ordering him out. Her face flushed and her very authoritative voice startled him, not because he shouldn't have been there, but because the sound of Andrew's voice commanded private conversation. He moved over to annoy another trader for information.

"I made a mistake in marrying Jean. I never should have." Andrew's voice rang in her ears. Lights on the trading desk flashed neon-like, salesmen pushing through the glass doors.

The firm won the California school bond issue, and the noise and turmoil that went with bond awards filled the space. The work place dictated Una's response. An average call during bid time lasted only a few minutes, and without thinking she spoke.

"Andrew, if you really love me, you will never call me again." She clicked back the black button on the board and pushed in another, starting to take bond orders.

It didn't take too long after five o'clock to get out the bond confirmations and the daily bulletin. The steno pool had a full staff working, and the issue was the only one the firm won.

Una had no time to think about Andrew's phone call until the long ride home on the subway. She pushed through the turnstile of the Wall Street subway station. The crowds had thinned out by now. The heat remained oppressive, but the air-conditioned office had a lingering effect on her body. A month had passed since that night in City Island. Una had noticed no physical change on her flat stomach; her secret remained. As she sat in her seat headed for home, his voice and words, "I made a mistake," echoed in a chamber-like dream sequence. *Did he really call? Did I dream it? No, he had called; remember, you told Mr. Rudman to get out.* That was a first for you. Her mother was right. He hadn't been married two months. *Poor Jean. Poor Jean, hell! Poor Una.* She wondered if his wife was pregnant too. Who cares, she has the ring on her finger. The ring, the almighty symbol. *Why does that symbol mean so much to me and not to him?* Una remembered when her mother found out about his engagement to Jean.

"Second best," her mother said. "Why are you settling for second best?"

"Ma, he's not married," she remembered saying. "He's only engaged and is waiting for the right moment to break the engagement." Well, now he was married and that ring meant something: hands off, forbidden territory. Solemn vows, that's what a wedding ring symbolized. *Does he think I'll go down the same road twice? Like hell I will. This baby will be better off being raised by a couple who truly want a baby. I wouldn't marry him. Wait a minute*, she thought, *you don't even have that option. What you would be is a mistress with his child. Forget it. What nerve. My mother was right; I'm too good for him.*

"It's too hot to eat, Ma; I'll just have some iced tea," Una called from her bedroom as she stripped out of work clothes and donned a pair of shorts and a blouse.

"You've got to eat. I made potato salad. I knew you wouldn't eat anything hot so the chicken is cold, too. I cooked it this morning and let it cool so as we could have a cold supper."

"Maybe later," Una poured a glass of iced tea from the pitcher and headed for the back porch, her mother close on her heels.

"I love it when your father is on the four to twelve shift."

"Why?"

Oh, I guess it's peaceful, especially at dinner time when you come home and we have time to talk and there's no chance of the McSweeney's dropping by unexpectedly."

"You're right about that; those people seem to think this is their second home."

"Well, it's not entirely the McSweeneys' fault. Your father enjoys ol' McSweeney's company. They have been friends for such a long time, and he likes entertaining them. It reminds him of home, I guess."

Una wondered if this would be a good time to share her secret with her mom. Why not? Her father wasn't there. She couldn't keep this from her mother much longer, and the fact that Andrew had called seemed to increase the urgency. She decided to share her pregnancy with her mother.

"Mom, remember how I carried on when I found out Andrew was getting married?"

"How could I forget that? You broke your heart crying and moping around for weeks, months."

"Well, him getting married was part of it, but, well, I'm going to have a baby."

"Dear mother of God! No. You're sure? Are you sure child? When could have this happened?"

"You remember the night I went to City Island on that big dinner date. Well, we had more than dinner that night. He bought champagne, and I guess I drank too much and he convinced me that he loved only me and well…." Una's voice trailed off and she looked down, not being able to face her mother.

"The bugger, the lying, rotten bugger, shaming you this way, shaming our family." She broke down in tears.

"Ma, don't carry on so, it will be all right. I've decided to put the baby up for adoption. Don't worry."

"Don't worry, you say, wait 'til your father finds out. There'll be hell to pay. I dread telling him."

"Maybe we won't have to."

"How's that?"

"Well, Uncle Conrad has not been too well. Daddy knows Aunt Ellen and he have been pestering for me to visit after Tim spent time with them before going into the seminary. This could be the perfect time if all goes well in my ad placement for the baby's adoption."

"It seems all of a sudden. Do you think we could do it? I really don't want him to know. There's no telling what he would do when some night he's on the ran dan. He would try and do something foolish and get himself into a lot of trouble."

"I'll have to put an ad in the personals column looking for a couple to finance the trip to Australia and pay for all my medical expenses."

"Before you do that, darling, I'll have to write and tell Ellen about your predicament."

"I guess you're right, Ma." Her mother got up from the chair, walked over to her daughter, and hugged her.

"I'm glad you told me and didn't try and do anything foolish." By now she had stopped crying and realized that Una's choice didn't end in her seeking to abort the child and perhaps jeopardize her own life. Una's mother turned and walked into the kitchen, gathering the dinner things as she went. As she stood in front of the sink, a cockroach scurried back into the crevice separating the caulking her husband had filled in a week ago. "Those lots next door, nothing but garbage and trash; can't get rid of those horrible creatures no matter what we do." The shock of Una's news jolted her own hidden past.

"I'm not going and that's that." Bridget stormed downstairs to her Aunt Sheilah's shop. Bridget and Patrick O'Connor had been married only a year and living in Glasgow, Scotland. Bridget came to Glasgow because she wanted to experience city life and get away from the farm in Donegal, Ireland. Her Aunt Sheilah had offered her a place in her home. Her husband had passed away and she was alone. She had no children of her own, but she did have a thriving sweet shop and offered Bridget a job. It wasn't long before she met Patrick O'Connor at one of the weekly dances in Maryhill. After a brief courtship they married, and Sheilah allowed them to stay on in the apartment over the store. Bridget helped out in the shop, and Patrick held down a job as a tram conductor.

Soon after the marriage, Patrick started to receive mail from an old friend of his, Hugh McSweeney. He loved working and living in New York City and was preparing to go to Delehanty's to learn the trade of stationary engineer. These letters fired up Patrick's adventurous nature to migrate to the United States, but Bridget liked the life she just started to get used to.

"Sure it's only a year's course Hugh said, and then you're guaranteed a job. I can't see myself driving a tram up and down Maryhill Road for the rest of my life."

Sheilah didn't like the idea much either. She would miss her niece, and the thought of her going off to a place without the security and comfort afforded them both didn't help Patrick's cause either. Most of their friends were divided about what they should do, and the arguments were beginning to frustrate the newlyweds. Patrick started staying out late after work and making the rounds of the pubs. When he came home, Sheilah would nag at him to make matters worse. He threatened to move out of her apartment Bridget realized a decision had to be made.

"I'll go to America," Bridget said, glaring at her husband across the dinner table one evening. "On one condition: you go on before, do your schooling, get a job, and have a place for me to come to. I can't see leaving Maryhill, Sheilah, and all my friends to go off to God knows what. Those are my terms, take them or leave them, and I'll hear no more of America."

Patrick, glad to hear part of the terms, didn't relish going on to the States without his wife, but he also knew the compromise was fair, so he agreed.

Soon after Patrick left for the States, Bridget got bored staying home after closing up the shop, so she started going back to the dances with her friends. It was at one of these dances she met Mickey Bradey, and oh, how he could dance a stack of barley. He was a charmer, and on more than one occasion he offered to escort her home.

In the beginning, she declined, but as the weeks went on her friends said she was foolish not to let him accompany her home. She missed her husband, and when he brushed up against her during some of the dances, hormones started racing.

One night on the way home a terrible rain storm came up and they had to take shelter in an old abandoned shirt factory. Both of them were soaked before they reached the entrance to the building. They were no sooner in the building when Mickey stripped to the waist, tossing his rain-soaked shirt with abandon. His hairy chest and bulging biceps reminded her of her husband.

"Here, take a swig; it will take the chill out." He reached into his back pocket and pulled out the flask. Reluctantly, she reached for it. "Too bad you can't get out of those wet clothes." Bridget, wet and cold, noticed him glare at her as she tossed back and gulped at the flask. The taste made her shake her head. "There now," he lowered his voice, "that should warm the cockles of your heart." Bridget stopped shivering.

"What's this?" He had stooped down to retrieve his wet shirt and his foot hit a huge object. Upon further examination he discovered the carton contained yards of shirt material left behind in the factory. "Well now," he smiled, "looks like we will have dry clothes after all." He laughed. He offered Bridget another swig of the flask and as she held it he pulled and tugged at the bolt of material in the box. "Here Bridget, make like a Greek."

In the dark she stripped and wrapped herself up in shirt cloth. By now the whiskey had relaxed her to a point where she was laughing along with Mickey. He, too, had removed his wet outer clothing and wrapped himself in a toga-like fashion.

Soon after this incident, Bridget found herself pregnant. Luckily, Sheilah calmed her down and offered a way out of her dilemma. Sheilah advised her not to say anything to anyone about the pregnancy, to stay in Glasgow until she started to show, and then to go back to Ireland. Everyone there would think it was very natural for her to want to get out of the city and settle for fresh air while awaiting the child. When the baby came, she would come back to Glasgow and leave the child for Sheilah to raise. It was a solution to her problem. Her husband would never know, because from his letters, she could tell he wanted nothing to do with the "old country."

The screen door slammed shut. "Want some help with the dinner things?" Una asked as she entered the small kitchen. The mosquitoes are winning the war out there; I think I'll hit the hay, Mom." She pecked her mother on the cheek, and her mother didn't say anything or turn around. Her watery eyes would have begged answers and they had nothing to do with Una's pregnancy.

Chapter Three

"We'll talk about it tonight; I'm running late." He turned and picked up his briefcase on the table by the front door, and Julia heard the door slam shut after him. Julia sulked at the kitchen table as the maid offered her another cup of coffee. She placed her hand over the cup. He was always late for something when she had something important to discuss. Julia and Clifford, both in their middle twenties and in excellent health, had been married for four years. They didn't have children and both were disappointed. Neither of them thought there would be any problem bringing children into the world, especially when they had a chance of having their own child.

A year before the wedding Julia had had an abortion. She hadn't considered this option when she found herself pregnant, but Clifford had convinced her it wouldn't look right if they hurried a wedding where a date had been set already; people would talk. The potential gossip didn't bother Julia as much as it did Clifford. Julia's father liked Clifford and had showed this by promoting him to general manager of his thriving newspaper soon after his arrival at the daily publication.

"Would you like to dance?" The blond, tanned young man asked Julia. The Corinthian Yacht Club's dance floor vibrated to the beat of a reggae band. She hadn't seen him approach her as her back was to him. Clifford noticed her as soon as Julia, her father, and mother entered the club. The family owned a home on the outskirts of Boston in Marblehead, and every fourth of July they came up for the yachting races. Clifford, along with several of his college classmates, rented a summer house just yards away. Both year-round and summer residents looked forward to the annual race and the black tie event that followed.

"Yes," she smiled back, and the two sailed off to the dance floor.

"Handsome," whispered her mother.

"It's the tan," Julia's father shot back. That evening began a courtship, and when Julia found out he worked as an editor for the *Boston Post*, she immediately dangled Clifford in front of her father at any given opportunity.

"Are you sure he didn't check out who you were before you two met?"

"Dad, how awful of you. You don't trust anyone; you've been in the news business too long," Julia whined. "All I'm saying is why don't you offer him a job on the paper? Chances are he just may refuse."

"I guess you will pester me until I do. But remember, if I feel he isn't right for the paper, I'm not going to hire him."

"Deal," And with that Julia hugged her father and bounded down the stairs to the waiting car at the curb.

The night following that conversation, Clifford found himself sharing a drink on the front porch with Julia's dad while she purposely delayed herself upstairs.

"So, Julia tells me you are an editor for the *Boston Post*. Do you intend to stay up in the New England area?"

"Well, for awhile. I want to get some experience before I head for the tri-state area."

"I've read your column; you're quite good. I especially like your biographical sketches on people in the news. Shows excellent research on your part."

"Thanks, I try to be thorough."

"How would you feel about writing a column for the *Shore Journal*? I've created a new department in Freehold. It's an area west of the shore and I'm looking for someone who is looking to advance a journalism career. Julia tells me you have worked as an intern while in school and graduated *cum laude*. Very impressive credentials. Think it over, we will be here until August One. You can let me know by then."

"What have you two been up to?" Julia rolled her eyes and smiled at Clifford.

"Business, dear, simply business," came her father's reply. Clifford placed the empty glass on the table, grabbed Julia's hand, and raced down the stairs. The night's oppressive humidity automatically headed the two toward the beach.

"I'll never get used to these rock beaches up here," Julia said, slipping and sliding on the stones. Clifford laughed and caught her around the waist as she lost her balance. "I'll be glad to see sand again and real soon; now tell me what you talked about." After he told her, she badgered him. "Well, what do you think? It would be a promotion; you would run the Freehold office in no time at all." She didn't give him a chance to reply but kissed him passionately on the lips.

Clifford didn't think it would bode well with Julia's father if the wedding date had to be moved up. Mr. Clark's life revolved around his only child and he had planned an elaborate event on the grounds of his home on the Jersey shore. Mr. Clark ran a tight ship. There were very few times, if any, when Mr. Clark's plans were altered because of others.

Julia had grown up observing her mother constantly deferring to her father's demands. There were never any loud arguments, but she did remember long bouts of silences between them. As a child, Julia had played with her dolls, telling them that if she ever married she would never stop talking to her husband. One time in particular stood out in her mind. She had been about seven or eight years old. The house seemed like a morgue. The painful childhood memory re-emerged when Clifford emphasized to Julia how upset her father would be about changing the wedding plans.

For years it had been traditional to go to Connecticut for the Thanksgiving holiday at her Aunt Theresa's house. Julia loved going and seeing cousins, and the beautiful New England countryside and riding horses. For some reason that year, her father decided that he would like to have Thanksgiving at home. Both Julia and her mother objected, but Mr. Clark remained resolute in his decision. Aunt Theresa tried to persuade her sister to come and to bring Julia if Clifford refused her, but Julia's mother couldn't bring herself to do that. Julia remembered the silence between them until Christmas Day of that particular year.

Both of them were young, he would remind Julia, they would have lots of babies. And what about disappointment to her father, he constantly reminded her. Their wedding date had been set; preparations were all in place. Julia couldn't deny she wanted all these things, but an abortion—she couldn't shake loose the implications the word intoned. But Clifford won that round. She often wondered, after they were married, if he ever thought of that horrible trip to Maryland, the dingy room in the boarding house where her baby's life had ended up in suction-like apparatus.

The day Clifford and Julia left for Maryland, they told her parents that one of her bridesmaids had invited them to visit for the weekend. Julia had sworn Olivia to secrecy, and Olivia had offered her home as a place for her to recuperate.

"Did you tell your mother anything? Olivia asked as Julia unpacked her things in one of the guest rooms.

"No, why upset her? Clifford thought the fewer people who knew the better off we would be."

"He's right, I suppose. Anyway, it will be all over tomorrow, and you can get on with the wedding." Olivia hung a dress of Julia's in the closet. Julia sat on the bed and started to cry.

"I really don't want to do this…but Clifford seems to think it best. Maybe he's right. I know how my father hates changes in plans of his, but I can't help but feel he just may, just may be able to accept *this*…I don't know."

She turned away and sobbed into the bedclothes. Her friend leaned over her, placing both hands on her back, and Julia turned and clung to her friend.

The next morning Clifford and Julia arose early with the excuse that they wanted to get some sightseeing done. After walking a few blocks away from Olivia's house they hailed a cab.

"You sure you want to go down there?" said the cab driver. "It's not the best neighborhood in the world." His words made Julia lace her arm into Clifford's and he patted it down.

"Yes, we do," Cliff replied and the cab sped away. The cab driver had been right in his remark. They saw a grimy three-story brick building with a garbage-littered stone stairway leading to a wood panel door. Cliff paid the cab driver while Julia clung to his coat sleeve. They ascended the stairs, rang the bell, and a bearded man opened the door.

"Are you the Browns?" the unshaven man asked.

"Yes," answered Cliff.

"One flight up, door on the left."

"Oh, Cliff," Julia whispered into his ear as she turned to look at the peeled paint on the walls and stumbled on the torn carpet on the stairs.

"It will be all right, Julia; I'm right here." Somehow his words did not lessen her fright.

When they reached the landing, a door to the right opened and a young woman exited, avoiding their eyes. Both Cliff and Julia moved to one side to let her pass and then they entered the room. Cliff was instructed to stay there while Julia was led down a hall into a smaller room with a reclining chair and stirrups on either side. A woman assisted her up after she removed her clothes and put on a hospital-type gown. She couldn't wait until the procedure was all over. She felt like she was going to the electric chair.

The first year after they were married Julia visited a gynecologist. He told her he could find nothing physically wrong with her and perhaps time would alter her non-parent status. Many newlyweds who want to get pregnant right away, he said, are sometimes too tense. This could cause problems for conception. She wanted to ask about the abortion causing any damage, but since he found nothing physical wanting, Julia opted to remain silent; besides, it was against the law, and by now she had inherited her father's newspaper and how would that look on the front page of the *Shore Journal*.

Her father died shortly after the wedding. Some people said the excitement of her wedding coupled with the daily pressure of the newspaper business took its toll on the energetic dynamo. He suffered a massive heart attack and died within hours. Her mother, devastated by the event, fell into a serious depression, and because of it Julia decided to move back into the rambling shore house she grew up in rather than build the house that she and

Cliff had planned on.

Clifford took over the job as publisher, and circulation increased rapidly. He expanded news coverage to the Freehold area and also had Washington reports covered on a daily basis. The paper took on a new dimension because of the creative changes he made, and now he, just like her father before him, had little time for domestic problems. *But this time he will listen*, Julia told herself. She was tired of the rejections they had received by adoption agencies over the past three years. *Wait* was a favorite word used at these places. You are young; give yourself some time. The word *wait* should be imprinted on adoption agencies letterhead. Sometimes at mass she prayerfully asked for forgiveness for her abortion and prayed for a miracle of some sort. And when she spied Una's ad in the *New York Times Sunday Edition*, she believed this might be her only chance at having a baby.

"Look, Cliff," she shouted as she read the ad giving the details and phone number to call. "This sounds too good to be true."

"Wait a minute, don't get so excited." Clifford's reaction was not what Julia had wanted. "You don't know anything about the mother or the father of this baby. There could be a lot of obstacles. For instance, are both parents white? I don't want to raise a child of mixed races." Julia's joy shattered; she never considered herself a bigot, but in her excitement she never gave thought to the father's race, Since the ad said *white female* she automatically assumed the father would be white too.

"I suppose you're right, but I want to call the number, though I can't until tomorrow, according to the paper."

"Suit yourself," he said and was gone. She rose from the chair and heard the maid talking to her mother about putting a chaise lounge on the back patio. *Should I mention this to my mother or should I wait a while? I'll wait*, she thought, *No need to involve Mother until I'm sure of what is going to happen.*

The cab pulled up and Una could smell the salt air. "That's 2 Passaic Avenue across the street." The cab driver offered to turn around, but Una said not to bother. She paid him and crossed the huge boulevard street. The Clarks' house sat on the corner at a right angle facing the ocean. A wraparound three-foot brick wall extended the length of the entire house, and a wrought iron gate leading to the main entrance gave one access. Una fiddled with the latch that brought to mind a scene out of the Dickens novel *Great Expectations*—the scene where Pip had been summoned to Ms. Haversham's, not knowing what to expect. Unlike Pip, who spent a lifetime trying to uncover his benefactor, Una somehow knew the fate of her unborn child would be decided that afternoon.

A short walk led to a flight of brick stairs ending in a massive stone wraparound with Ionic columns facing out from the house. While waiting for someone to open the great oak door, she turned on her high heels to view the ocean. *What a beautiful, powerful sight*, she thought to herself. *Imagine being able to look at this every time you came out the front door.* It sure beat the back fences of Kelly Street the O'Connor's viewed from their back porch. The door swung open, and a slender black woman dressed in all black with the exception of a white apron asked her, "Are you Miss O'Connor? The Clarks have been expecting you." The maid motioned for Una to come in.

Standing in what appeared to be the lobby of Radio City Music Hall in New York, Una absent-mindedly said out loud, "My what a big house," and then walked over and sat in one of the several couches in the living room. The high ceilings flowed into a circular stairway that had a pulpit-like side. Una had never been in such opulence. Soon a young blond woman, not much older than Una, appeared on the landing of the stairway. *She's gorgeous*, thought Una and overheard her telling the maid to bring in some tea.

"Hello Miss O'Connor, or shall I call you Una?" Julia said smiling.

"Una is fine, Mrs. Clark."

"Oh, please call me Julia. This must be very difficult for you," Julia said.

"Yes, it is, but I feel better now that we've met. You're not much older than I."

"Were you really expecting someone old?" Julia asked puzzled.

"Well, I really don't know what to have expected. Perhaps it never occurred to me that some young woman can have problems not having children. I suppose because I only did it one ti..." her voice trailed off.

"I understand, Una" Julia said, interrupting and helping her out of an embarrassing situation. "You said you would like to go to Australia to have the baby. May I ask why?"

Julia moved a small Roman bust to one side so the maid could set the tea down on the table.

"Well, it's a long story. The father of my baby is unaware. He is married, but if I could would like to save my family the embarrassment. I have an aunt and uncle who life in Sydney."

"I see; do you take sugar, milk?" she asked fussing over the tea things. *Why can't she have children?* thought Una as she answered the questions about sugar and milk. *She's so young.* "My husband and I will have to make arrangements as well to go to Australia. When do you expect the baby?"

"Some time in February, according to my calculations." Una sipped her tea.

"Well, that makes you about three months pregnant. You certainly don't look it."

"It's the clothes I wear. It's amazing how you can conceal things when you're forced to."

"The father, could you tell me something about him?"

"Quite handsome, medium height, blue eyes, very athletic, he played baseball for awhile, even made the Yankee farm team until he contracted yellow jaundice."

"Oh," Julia reacted to the last remark with surprise. "Was he sick long?"

"For about a year, but he did make a complete recovery. Is there going to be a problem with the baby being sick?"

"I don't know; that's something a doctor would have to answer. Have you seen a doctor yet?"

"No, I was waiting until after I met you and we decided that the adoption would go through. I have told my mother but not my father. I felt that if I knew what I intended to do it would help me in determining what options I have. Going to Australia would alleviate telling my father. My aunt's husband has been recovering from a heart condition, and I could say I wanted to visit them and help out in their store. They own a clock shop in Sydney. I could take a leave of absence from my job. In this way my mother would have to be the only one to know."

"I would like you to meet my husband; perhaps after you went to the doctor you could visit again, and if there is no problem we could arrange financial arrangements for your travel. Meanwhile, I suggest you inquire about the cost of the trip and other medical expenses you might incur. Of course, you will have to tell your aunt and uncle. Will that create a problem?"

"My aunt and uncle are very fond of me. They have no children of their own, and since my brother's visit before he left for the seminary, they have pestered me to visit as well. Ever since we were little, Tim and I have corresponded regularly with them, and I know I will feel comfortable with them during this pregnancy. More than if I stayed at home."

"Well then," Julia got up indicating the visit had come to a close, "I'll be expecting a call from you soon after you have seen a doctor and explained the circumstances. I would like to know about your progress and if the father's jaundice is any reason for concern."

"I'll be in touch. You have the right to know as much as possible about me and this baby." Julia stood, walked toward the front door, and Una followed. Julia opened the door and Una realized what a breathtaking view of the ocean the lady of the house had. The interview was over.

The massive door closed behind Una. Julia, inside of the house, smiled and started humming. She thought, *What a beautiful young woman. I will have a beautiful baby, if the father is as handsome as she is pretty, the baby should be gorgeous. His blue eyes should put Cliff at ease about race too.* I wonder, she thought *if it ever crossed her mind to have an abortion? But then, she said the father is unaware of her condition. Lucky for her; he probably would have done what Cliff offered me.* The memory of lying sweating profusely in a darkened room, wanting to run from the procedure about to be performed on her. No, this time she would be in charge of running her life, and Clifford would just have to take a back seat. There was more at stake here than partaking of a traditional holiday dinner.

Una glanced at her watch. The train back to New York wasn't until three fifteen. She had an hour to wait. She thought to walk the boards but remembered the cab had driven past a small business district. She turned, inhaled the fresh air, and headed toward town.

Chapter Four

"Who could be calling at this time of night?" Mrs. O'Connor mumbled, stumbling down the darkened hallway to the dining room and past her daughter's bedroom. The phone's relentless ringing echoed loudly in the stillness of the night.

Just as she reached the entrance to the dining room, Una's bedroom door opened and she too stepped into the hallway.

"Ellen, is that you?" Mrs. O'Connor now wide awake, she held the receiver to her ear. "Oh no, when…when did this happen?" Una knew from the color of her mother's face, which by now had turned ash white, and by the tone of her voice that her Uncle Conrad had died. Tears streamed down her face and Una rushed to her side, wrapping herself around her. "Yes, I'll try and come as soon as possible." Her mother put the receiver down and burst into convulsive sobs. Both women cried for a long while.

"There's your father home," said Mrs. O'Connor as she heard the front door open and close. By now both women had gone into the kitchen, talking in somber tones about the suddenness of Conrad's death. Now they were discussing the effect his death would have on Una's dilemma.

"How could you possibly go to the funeral, Ma? Tim's ordination is next week?"

"I never thought of that," said her mother, still shaken by the bad news.

"I could go in your place, Ma. This way I could get a leave of absence from my job, and it would work out that Daddy wouldn't know about the baby. You said they were both happy about me going over to visit, and there would be no problem about my condition. I could help out at the store and be company for Aunt Ellen as well."

"What are you two up for at this hour of the night?" Mr. O'Connor said, pulling off his shirt. Glancing at the ashen faces of his wife and daughter, he knew that something was terribly wrong. "What is it? Did something happen to Tim? Who died?"

"Tim is fine, It's...Conrad. He passed away early this morning. Ellen called and asked if I could come over, and without thinking I said yes. But Tim's ordination is next week, so Una said she would go in my place. There would be no trouble for her to get a leave of absence from her work. So that's that." Mrs. O'Connor again went into a fit of sobbing.

"The poor bugger, he worked so hard to get that shop going, and just when it is showing some kind of profit...." Una stared at her father who by now enveloped his wife in a bear hug. How different this scene was from one she witnessed some years ago.

"Shh, you'll wake the children." Una's parents had come home from a local Irish dance.

"Don't shh me," he incoherently spit out the words and reeled back toward the kitchen window. "What did that Mickey Bradey mean by, 'remember the shirt factory'? Come on now, answer up." The level of their voice woke both Una and Tim. Tim rushed into the small kitchen just in time to come between his father's raised hand and his mother's face.

Tim grabbed his father's hand and spun him backwards against the kitchen window. In his drunken stupor he staggered and fell on the floor. Una pulled her mother into the hallway and led her into the dining room. Once there Una closed the door and tried to calm her mother.

"Oh, it was awful, just awful," her mother cried.

"What ever happened to make Daddy so mad at you? I have never seem him so worked up. What happened at the dance?"

In between her mother's sobs, Una made out a name: Mickey Bradey. This man made some offensive remark to her mother and when she tried to explain it away as the remark of an unruly lout, it made matters worse. The two men involved themselves in a brawl right in the middle of the dance floor.

"What did this man, this Mickey Bradey, say that got him so riled up?" Her mother avoided the question putting her head back down into her hands and started sobbing again. "There, there," Una consoled her mother. "I hate when he drags you down to 138th Street to those horrible dance halls. Why don't you refuse to go? You yourself said there's nothing but drunken brawls nowadays, and nobody worth their salts would go."

"I know," her mother said, still crying, "but if I don't go with him there's no telling when he would come home."

Tim had helped his father into bed and removed his clothing. His father kept repeating, "That lying bugger Mickey Bradey. I'll kill him for the things he said bout your mother, the bastard."

"OK, Dad maybe tomorrow, but for now have a sleep so you'll be up to it." By now Una had made up the couch in the living room for her mother to retire and she came into the kitchen just as Tim closed the bedroom door.

"Boy, I wonder who this Mickey Bradey is?" Tim said to Una as she put the kettle on for tea.

"Want a cup of tea? I'm wide awake now; maybe the tea will help us get back to sleep. Oh, some drunken bum, who mouthed off at Mom. Probably had her mixed up with one of the regulars who goes to the dances. Who knows. I just wish she wouldn't go there. Mom says years ago there was a lot more dancing and not much drinking. Now it seems to be the reverse."

"I don't think Mom will be going anymore," said Tim. "At least I'd advise her not to, and if she can convince Dad as well, it would be better for both of them to find another place for the dances."

Una poured the tea for the two of them and they sat a while talking about Tim's dream to enter the seminary that fall. She wondered what in the world she would ever do without her "peacemaker" of a brother after he was gone.

After Una's interview with Julia Clark she had made an appointment with a gynecologist. Una found out her baby's due date was February 14. Everything appeared normal and the yellow jaundice the father had would not have an adverse effect on the infant. Medical expenses were discussed, and Una explained that the baby would be born in Australia. The day after her visit to the doctor she called Julia Clark. Julia had asked her to visit again so she and her husband could meet. A date had been set for Una to visit with the Clarks at their home, but the urgent phone call received from her Aunt Ellen had changed all that.

"Mrs. Clark...Julia?" Una remembered they were talking on a first name basis. "We have had some bad news about my uncle in Australia. He suffered a massive heart attack, and my aunt has asked my mother to come to his funeral. My mother and I both have agreed this would be ideal for me to go in her place as my brother Tim will be ordained a priest next week and she wants to attend."

"I'm sorry to hear about your trouble. Meeting with my husband—" Her voice stopped mid-sentence. "He plans to be in New York tomorrow on business. Do you think you could meet him for lunch downtown?"

"I think that's possible. I'll give you my business phone number, and he can call me when he arrives in New York." Una gave her the number and tried to picture the man destined to be the father of her child.

Julia didn't look forward to having to face Clifford about the change in plans. From the beginning, he had doubted that this adoption had been in their best interest. If she didn't persist, he never would have agreed to meeting Una in the first place. Now, because of the death in Una's family, Julia had to ask him to meet a strange woman in New York who was carrying his future child. When Clifford argued with her that evening about the sudden rush, she quickly reminded him that, had she not agreed to listen to him about aborting their baby, things would have been entirely different and they would have their own child.

Reluctantly, he agreed to the meeting the next day.

He scanned the tables at the restaurant where he and Una were to have lunch. Una had suggested a restaurant right on Broadway off of Wall Street since Clifford had called that morning, mentioning his business appointment would be in that vicinity. She described the outfit she had on and asked if 12:00 noon would be all right. There she was *quite pretty*, he thought to himself as she zigzagged in and around tables.

"Hello, I'm Cliff Clark." He extended his hand as she moved the chair to sit down.

"Nice to meet you. Una O'Connor," she said. The table he had selected was just for two and as close to the back of the restaurant as he could get.

"I'm sorry to hear about your uncle," the handsome, tanned blond man said. Una knew his words to be devoid of any condolences, but they were in keeping with his demeanor and outward appearance.

"Thank you. But, not to sound cold and callous, my uncle's death has come at a time that makes it a lot easier for me. My father is under the impression I'm standing in for my mother. My brother, Tim, is going to be ordained next week, and my mother would never miss that ceremony. He has been in the seminary seven years and she has been looking forward to this day for some time."

While Una rambled on in answer to Clifford's inquires about who the father was and whether he knew she was pregnant, he couldn't help but hear the same edge in her voice that he had heard in his wife's the night before. This lovely pretty girl with a touch of freckles on the bridge of her nose was dealing with a situation Julia also had not too long ago. As they ate, Clifford discussed how his lawyer would draw up documents for Una to sign before she left and how he would set up a bank account in Sydney once she had settled there. After an hour and a half Una got up to leave for her office, satisfied with the outcome of meeting with the man who was securing a bright future for her child.

"Mr. Basset, may I see you for a moment?" Una said. She had decided to speak to the office manager as soon as she returned. She explained her uncle's sudden death and how she planned on attending the funeral because of certain circumstances, and asked would he secure a leave of absence for her from the firm immediately?

"I'll take care of that Miss O'Connor. And again may I offer my condolences to you and your family."

The rest of the afternoon, she made the rounds saying her goodbyes to her fellow employees. Questions abounded: "How long will you be gone?" "Was he sick long?" She felt relieved when five o'clock came, and there came and end to the charade of the real reason for her leaving.

Mart had been kept up to date on a daily basis during their subway rides to work.

"I'm going to miss you something awful," she lamented when Una called her that evening.

"Me, too," Una sighed into the phone. "I don't know how long I'll be gone. With my uncle not running the shop, I don't know what my aunt intends to do. But I would like to repay her in some way for allowing me to stay until the baby comes."

"How will it be when the baby comes? Will you come home with it or…?"

"No, Mrs. Clark—Julia is flying over to Sydney a week before the fourteenth of February, and she'll stay until the baby arrives and then take the baby home with her."

"Don't forget to write and tell me all about those awesome Aussies."

"I'll write, but as far as the awesome Aussies, I don't think they will have much interest in me," said Una matter-of-factly, then added, "or I in them."

She and Marta chatted on for a while, and then finally ended the conversation. Una stared at the phone after placing the receiver on its hook and thought to herself that yes, she will surely miss her dearest friend and all the dreams they had shared with each other over the years. She turned and went into her room to finish packing. Her flight to Sydney was out of Kennedy Airport the day after tomorrow.

Chapter Five

It had been snowing all morning. The nun realized an impact on freshman orientation. Orientation had been scheduled for 10:00 A.M., but when she reached Cabrini Hall soon after the hour there was not a freshman in sight.

She walked up to the podium set up for the event and checked the papers on the stand to make sure the list of incoming names could be checked against the students reporting. As she glanced down the list, her eyes stopped at the name *Bridget Clark, Spring Lake, NJ*. Could it be? Her body felt faint, she grasped the podium to regain her composure. Memories of years before swirled in her brain like the snowflakes just outside of Cabrini Hall.

The kaleidoscope aroused emotions of long ago. Feelings of passionate lovemaking in the back seat of a car some twenty years ago emblazoned her being, lovemaking that conceived a child that night. The betrayal, Andrew's marriage to Jean, the phone call saying he had made a mistake, trips to the Clarks, the death of her uncle, the trip to Australia, and finally Bridget's birth. *Has it been that long?* She thought to herself. Marta's wedding soon after she returned from Australia, finishing Fordham and attaining a master's degree in education, changing careers from finance to teaching. Yes, it had been that long ago.

In the early years of her teaching, especially at the elementary level, she would fantasize about her daughter. Little girls of six or seven allowed her the luxury to daydream of what could have been. The progression of the children moving along to the upper grades stabilized her, and the constant stream of new students soon dulled her early fantasies. Una found herself totally consumed with teaching and decided to enter a teaching order of nuns. She had remembered her brother, Tim, and his wonderful counseling during this decision-making process.

"It's not for everyone," he cautioned Una when she approached him about entering the convent.

"I suppose you think I'm running away and hiding in a convent because I'm not married."

"It did cross my mind." He smiled.

"Well, no. Ever since I came home from Aunt Ellen's, I have felt different about what I'd like to do with my life."

"What do you mean?"

"Teaching…I love teaching. In fact I find it consumes most of my time. Working with students and watching them learn, grow, and discover their own way gives me the utmost pleasure, more than I ever received at my job on Wall Street. There, it had been a rat race, and I didn't appreciate the perks some of the men bestowed on me while on the job…if you know what I mean."

"You could teach without becoming a nun."

"Yes, I know, but somehow I feel this is something I would like to explore."

On that thought reality brought Sister Calista back to Cabrini Hall.

The canyon room started to fill up with girls. *Could I pick her out of a crowd?* Sister Calista's eyes scanned the bone-chilled students, some shaking snow off their outer clothing. She didn't have the luxury to study each and every one, because the students filling the seats had their eyes focused on her in expectation of a welcome.

"The College of New Rochelle welcomes each and every one of you," she began. During orientation program she elaborated for an hour on the rules and regulations. At the end of the address, she did something she normally didn't do. She asked each student if she would stand, give her name, and say what type of program she hoped to pursue. After the fifth student, a brown-haired teenager stood, "Bridget Clark, pre-law," she said. Her mother's name, Bridget, resounded in Una's mind long after all the other students had declared themselves. Her mother's name had been the only tie to her baby. Julia Clark conceded many years ago that she would comply with the only request Una had made, and that had been to name her child.

Orientation had come to a close, and the students started to file out of the hall and across the quad to the cafeteria for lunch. The snow had stopped and the freshman enjoyed the trek, laughing and striking up conversations as they plowed their way to the nearby building. Sister Calista followed the group and upon arrival inside scanned the tables to see where Bridget had alighted. After fixing her tray, she headed straight for the table with the group of students that included her daughter.

"Mind if I sit here?" She smiled at the girls.

"No, not at all," one of the freshmen volunteered. Bridget now was directly across from her. Trying not to stare but drinking in the sight of her daughter's lovely blue eyes—that definitely reminded her of Andrew—her lightly freckled complexion, a perfect smile that showed gleaming white teeth, she proceeded to prod into her study course.

"So, what made you choose the College of New Rochelle—and your course of study, pre-law if I remember rightly?"

Bridget looked with surprise at her. "You must have a fabulous memory, with all the girls and choices mentioned, to remember." Her voice trailed off with a shocked look at the nun across the table from her.

"Not really." *The child is right*, she thought. *You better come up with a clever response.* "I have an ulterior motive. I coach the debating team, and I'm always on the lookout for potential debaters, pre-law students are prime targets." she laughed.

"Oh, well, then I'm sure we will be seeing a great deal of each other." Bridget explained how she started at Lehigh the previous September but the co-ed atmosphere led to too much partying. "I'm serious about learning and the dorm parties every weekend were just too much for me, so I thought I'd try an all-girls college with a strong pre-law curricula, especially labor law, so here I am."

"Why labor law? Did you parents suggest that type of career for you?"

"No, my father is a publisher. If anything, both my parents would have loved it if I had chosen a journalism career, but somehow or other I've felt a pull toward the study of the law. Ever since I was a kid I have had this social consciousness—things bothered me, like the environment." She started to laugh as childhood memories abounded. "Like the time when I was in the sixth grade, I started an ecology club called Blue Gamma. I liked to read biographies…I read Jane Adams when I was about twelve and how she started Hull House in Chicago. I was impressed how she accompanied her wealthy father when he traveled in the slums on the outskirts of Chicago and vowed she would do something about it when she grew up."

And *here she is all grown up*, her mother thought, *and ready to take on the world much like I did when I was her age.* Her daughter's reminiscences echoed an important conversation between an old boss and herself.

"You'll get married as soon as the training period is over," Mr. Rockwell, the director of the municipal department, said. "The firm would have invested time and money in training you and then you would get married, have a baby, and you would be gone."

"I have no intention of getting married, at least not for a long time. I'm not even going with anyone at the moment. Please just let me have a chance. If I can't keep up, or am impossible to train, you can let me go…I'll go back and work in the bond cages."

"I don't know…anyway there are no vacancies at present. I'll keep in mind what you had said, and if there should be need of another trader I'll give it some thought." The interview was over.

"Too bad I didn't have you negotiating my salary when I held my first job. Back in the late fifties and early sixties women seldom attempted to venture into a male-dominant position. I had the wonderful experience of trading municipal bonds on Wall Street for a number of years and enjoyed it immensely. I loved my work so much I never realized I was taken advantage of…money-wise, that is. I knew the men I worked with made more money than I, but because I loved what I did and as long as my salary kept up with the salaries of women who were leaving the typing pool and working their way up the corporate ladder as private secretaries, it didn't bother me."

"That's terrible." Bridget's eyes widened." No wonder women revolted; what you just told me is the reason women have rebelled against the establishment."

"I suppose you're right, but you must remember I knew the money wasn't the same and I also knew that Mr. Rockwell, who was the head of the department, knew. In his way he compensated by giving me Mondays and Fridays off during the summer because I had rented a summer house at the Jersey shore with two other girls."

The Jersey shore appealed to Sister many years ago, when she first visited the Clarks. Upon her return from Australia, she, along with two secretaries, spent summer months commuting back and forth to New York. "This arrangement didn't bode too well with the other male traders, but Mr. Rockwell made this decision, and I felt this was more than equitable. It certainly made for wonderful long weekends during the summer, and I enjoyed it immensely."

"So you have been in my neck of the woods," Bridget smiled.

I better stop reminiscencing right now, before I blurt out she is my daughter. The cafeteria help were stacking chairs on the tables and the noise helped end the conversation.

"Yes, I have—but that's a discussion for another time. I think we'd better get out of here and let them clean up. The dates for sign-ups on the debating team will be posted in Cabrini Hall at the end of the week. See you then." Bridget headed up to her dorm assignment and Sister Calista to administration.

There had been no sign-ups the first hour. Sister Calista spread paperwork out on the desk where she sat, making use of the down time awaiting students interested in joining the debating club. She glanced at her watch: another forty-five minutes to go. Two seniors, her best debaters, had been scheduled to graduate in June, and she would have to move her two alternates up to "varsity level." If she didn't get any replacements, it would leave the team under a great deal of pressure in the event anyone got sick or had conflicting class schedules.

"Hello, Sister." Sister looked up at the door slowly opening and two women entered the room.

"Come in, come in." She rose from the chair and walked over to greet the students. "I was just wondering if anyone had seen the sign about registration. You're the first sign-ups. I know you, Miss Clark. And you are?"

"Patricia Morley. I'm a political science major. Bridget kind of talked me into trying out. She believes if I'm into politics, I'm going to be giving a great deal of speeches."

"She's right, you know. I have seen my students develop in their four years into self-assured speakers able to think quickly on their feet. The practice of using words to get your ideas across is a marvelous tool, especially in the fields both of you girls have chosen. On a lighter note, your showing up is a great relief to me because two of my students are scheduled to graduate this June. I always like to have alternates. It takes pressure off the team to know replacements are nearby in case of conflict with class scheduling."

"Glad to be of assistance," Bridget said, smiling. The girls filled out the necessary papers and were on their way.

Chapter Six

Winter dragged on well into spring, leaving mounds of snow in and around campus. One snowstorm followed another, keeping temperatures hovering low into the thirties for most of February and March. Sister Calista had been plagued with a nagging cough that hung on as stubbornly as winter did.

"When are you going to do something about that horrible cough of yours? Tim asked, as his sister put down the glass of water. Tim and Sister Calista were having dinner in a New York restaurant during the college's Easter recess after seeing the play *Da* at a matinee that Wednesday. He had given his sister two tickets at Christmas, and when he called to see if she was going, she complained she hadn't been feeling well.

"I'm trying to shake off a horrible cough, but yes, of course I'm going. In fact I've been looking forward to seeing you and the play. By next Wednesday I should be fine. I've made an appointment for next week; I just never seem to have the time to squeeze in doctors' appointments, but you're right, this has lasted a little too long to suit me. It's beginning to interfere with my work, especially in my debating duties."

"Good. Did you get any new recruits for the team? I know you had been worried about your two seniors leaving in June."

"Yes, two lovely girls. One is a pre-law student and the other a political science major." His sister wished she could have shared the happiness she felt with Tim about seeing her daughter on an almost daily basis. Tim and his sister had always been close, and now, with both their father and mother dead, their relationship became even closer with more frequent phone calls and visits. Sometimes she had wished she had shared her secret with her brother long before, but when she had left for Australia, she had believed it would have taken away from his special day and she didn't want to do that. He had studied so long and didn't deserve to be upset by her unexpected pregnancy.

"Good backup, at least if they steer the course in keeping to their chosen majors," her brother said.

"One of the girls, Bridget…is especially bright." Mentioning her daughter's name lit up her face and she continued excitedly, "She's the one who is pre-law. I'm kind of glad she joined the team. We're scheduled to debate next November in the Lincoln-Douglas competition at Georgetown University and the proposition is, 'Resolved: Should the Ruling of the Supreme Court Roe vs. Wade Be Overturned?'"

"That will keep them in a law library for hours," her brother said. "You know, a lot of people think that the Roe vs. Wade decision last year had a lot to do with the ERA amendment. Personally, I think that whole case was based on a couple of lawyers bent on winning a test case before the Supreme Court. Some lawyers down in Texas, who happened to be women, got hold of a poor, unfortunate pregnant woman and made an example of her by parading her through a state court. And timing was on their side."

"Oh, come on, now—those lawyers may have been misguided in their thinking, but really, I think they became emotionally involved with this women's plight and thought they could help her out. Why is it you men always think it's about winning?"

"Because I happen to have a friend, a lawyer, smart as they come. He was involved in the bishop's council to stop the New York state legislature from changing the existing abortion law on their books. After losing that round, he told me how he hated that case, but he knew that the evidence for abortion weighed heavily against the existing antiquated laws dealing with it."

"What do you mean?"

"Well, for one thing the Supreme Court's decision was based on the fact the judges were not presented with enough evidence as to when life begins."

"That's ridiculous. If a woman has intercourse and misses her period, she knows or at least suspects, she's pregnant and is going to have a baby."

"You know that and I know that, but these lawyers knew, with all the evidence collected, that a test case was just a matter of time. They were able to convince the Supreme Court that between 1967 and 1973, four states repealed their abortion laws. I can't think of all of them, but I know New York was one of them. In addition to medical documentation that couldn't indicate when a fetus became viable, and present-day lawsuits challenging criminal abortion, those lawyers had a field day. And I'm sure it looked good on their resumes, arguing before the Supreme Court of the United States and winning the case."

Tim leaned back in his chair, looking dejected, a look she knew well—a look of not being able to fix something, like when they were children and her doll's arm came off and he tried as best he could to reattach it in its socket but it just wouldn't stay.

"And I always thought that these lawyers taking all these cases were either doing it out of compassion for the women or the money it generated."

"Maybe four or five years ago that could have been the case, but there was a strong surge that came out of the sixties, the sexual revolution, if you will. The laws on the books should have been addressed. From what my friend told me, some of those laws made criminals out of doctors who helped to save women from bleeding to death after having an ectopic pregnancy."

"What's an ectopic pregnancy?"

"It's when the baby is growing outside the womb. Nature has a way of aborting the fetus, but in some cases, the woman needs medical help. Some of these laws needed to address situations such as these, but once abortions became legal, abortion on demand followed."

"I never knew you were so knowledgeable about this. I never knew about ectopic pregnancy."

"If it hadn't been for my friend, who filled me in on his daily research, I wouldn't have either."

"I remember attending some debates when the issue of abortion was headed for the New York state legislature. People there...and of course, most of them women...were making arguments about how it's time we stop back-alley abortions and women having to go to these butchers, and most of them were saying they only wanted abortions allowed in cases of rape and incest. When any other point was made by someone saying once abortions were allowed, abortion on demand would soon follow, they were shouted down. Who ever thought the Supreme Court would make such a ruling?"

"It's a sign of the times," her brother sighed. He called the waiter for the check. "We'll catch a cab; it'll give us plenty of time before our trains leave. We have about forty minutes."

The train ride back to the college had left Sister exhausted. She took fits of coughing, and it had gotten so bad at one time she actually got up because the woman next to her started pressing up against the window, fidgeting with her purse. *The doctor's next week, if not sooner*, she thought as she jostled down the aisle of the train and stood on the platform between the cars. The air had seemed a little fresher on the platform, and she inhaled deeply. When she thought the coughing spell had passed, she opened the door to the next compartment and started to look for a seat.

She thought about how good her brother looked and how wonderful it had been to see him. Although they kept in touch with weekly phone calls, being with him had been the highlight of her Easter vacation. The conversation they had over dinner replayed in her mind. *All that talk about abortion...? I never gave it a thought when I had been pregnant...but then again that had been the fifties...a lot of water under the bridge since then.* She pictured her daughter's face and smiled. There had been one thought of her brother's—the words about "winning a test case"—it reminded her of an incident of long ago, but she couldn't place just where. The train rattled on and she tried to sleep but to no avail, and when she finally arrived home she couldn't wait to down spoonsful of cough syrup, aspirins, and go to bed.

Upon rising the next morning, Tim's word's, "winning a test case," played over and over in her mind and conjured up a scene out of Sister Calista's past.

One of her very first teaching assignments after receiving her teaching certificate had been the fourth grade at a local public elementary school. The children had been assigned to write a composition about a hero they admired. One little boy had written about the famous football coach Vince Lombardi. The boy's obsession with football showed up in every word.

"My, this is a wonderful story about football. You certainly know a lot about the game. Where did you learn all this?"

"From a book I got from the library. Want to see it?"

"I would love to."

The child reached into his desk and handed her a picture book titled *Winning Is the Only Thing*. The book had been geared for a young male audience and emphasized the title throughout. Something bothered her about the author's zeal in conveying this message without any allowance for failure. It bothered her so much she started reading about the famous coach herself.

After reading a great deal about Vince Lombardi, it made her even angrier about the children's book that made its way into the hands of one of her students. The title had not even been original; it had been the last line of a speech the coach had given before a group of businessmen. Lombardi's ability to take a losing football team like the Green Bay Packers, turn it around so that it made the Super Bowl twice, and win both times made him a much sought-after speaker. However, this children's author missed completely Lombardi's own admission when at the height of his career, he publicly stated to the world, that the pressure of winning was torturing and he could no longer forgive himself a single defeat. He resigned from the Green Bay Packers in January 1968. His retirement didn't last, too, because he accepted the head coaching job for the Washington Redskins in 1969. Perhaps the cancer that killed him in November 1970 could have been linked to the stress and pressure of winning.

Funny how words can trigger a memory of so long ago and remember all its intricate details. *Well*, she thought to herself, *I would like to win the next debate in November but first things first.* She picked up the phone and rescheduled her doctor's appointment for that afternoon.

"Pat, wait up," Bridget called to her friend. The quads had been dotted with students headed for their respective dorms upon returning from Easter break. Bridget, upon seeing her friend getting out of the car in the parking lot, tried desperately to catch up with her but had been hampered with the excess baggage her mother insisted accompany her back to school—the "goody bag" her mother had called it. Her friend turned when she heard her name called and started to laugh out loud at the spectacle.

"What are you laughing at?" Bridget managed to blurt out after the sprint she made toward her friend.

"You…you look so funny trying to juggle all that stuff. What have you got there anyway?"

"Don't know, my mom packs her 'goody bag,' and I unpack it when I get here, and believe you me, it's greatly appreciated…you'll see…some night when you're looking for something to pig out on."

"In that case let me help you. Here, give me one of those bags. How was Easter vacation? I know I said I would try and visit you, but I got caught up with family and old friends and before I knew it, time to come back."

"It's just as well. My father had arranged an internship this summer down in Washington working for Senator Lautenberg, and he had scheduled interviews for me with his staff that week."

"How exciting, what kind of an internship is it?"

"I will be working with the New Jersey Environmental Lobby, sending out letters, making phone calls…at least that's the job description they told me."

"Will you be gone the entire summer?"

"Pretty much, I leave June 30th and will be back August 15th." The girls just about reached their dorms when Sister Calista came toward them.

"Hi girls," the nun smiled. "I've heard from the committee on the Lincoln-Douglas Debates and the proposition for the November debate."

"What is it?" both girls said in unison.

"Resolved; Should the ruling of the Supreme Court Roe vs. Wade Be Overturned?"

"That should make for interesting conversation around the dinner table," Bridget said. "At least in my house. My mother and father can't seem to agree about that decision."

"In what respect?" asked the nun.

"Well, my father seems to lean toward the decision of the Supreme Court but my mother is adamantly opposed to it."

"Your family is not the only one in turmoil about this. That's why it should be discussed and debated. My brother gave me some pertinent information I intend to share with the team before summer recess. It will be up to the team to do a great deal of research and come up with some ideas during the summer months. I'll be counting on them."

"Tell her, Bridget…tell her about where you will be for the summer and what you will be doing," her friend said.

"That's wonderful," the nun said after Bridget gave details of the

Washington internship. "What an opportunity all around…for experience in your major and access to all that research for the debate."

"Yes, I'm really looking forward to it."

Sister looked down at her watch. "Oh, I'm running late. I have a doctor's appointment. See you girls." Both girls disappeared into the dorm.

Chapter Seven

"When did you have pleurisy?" Doctor Edwards inquired as he probed with his stethoscope.

The instrument felt cold up against her back. His question puzzled her because she had begun to feel good. The antibiotics he had prescribed cleared up the nagging cough. When she received a call from his office to review results of x-rays, she expected to hear everything was fine.

"There is some scar tissue in your right lung," he pointed to an x-ray on a screen. "However, that's not what bothers me. Do you see this shadow in your left lung? I would like to examine it further. I would like to set up an appointment for a biopsy so we can rule out anything serious."

"What?" she said, staring at the x-ray. "I never had pleurisy." She raised her voice in defiance as if her words could erase what she saw before her eyes.

"You may think you have never had pleurisy, Sister, but the evidence is there. The body is a wonderful and sometimes baffling organism. It has the power to heal itself, and modern technology allows us to peek inside and see how it's done. Those scars on your lung could have been left there a long time ago...possibly as a child."

"Could the shadow in my lung be a recurrence of pleurisy?"

"I don't know. I can't answer that until I see the results of a biopsy."

The conversation between doctor and patient had been as cold and sterile as the stethoscope. "Why don't you get dressed, Sister? We'll set up an appointment for the surgery. See the receptionist at the desk."

Sister reached for her clothing. *This can't be happening to me—not now, when I have the opportunity for the next four years to be involved in Bridget's life.* She felt like crying. But no, that would have to wait until she was alone.

"Girls, I have some unsettling news." Sister had perched on the end of the desk and spoke to the debating team right after the visit to her doctor. "My doctor has determined from test results on my lungs that I'll have to have a biopsy. It's scheduled for next week, so today I would like to designate research areas to each of you."

"Oh, Sister Calista, how awful for you," one of the girls blurted while the others sat rigid in their seats, wide-eyed.

"Now, girls, until the results are in there is no need to panic," she said, trying to reassure herself as well as the girls. "I feel fine, but the doctor wants to check out some old scar tissue and rule out anything serious, so remember me in your prayers. She continued handing out research material for each of the girls to explore over the summer months.

"What did you get to look up, Bridget?" said Patricia, swinging her backpack up to her shoulders.

"The Court's decision on viability, how about you?"

"The right to privacy. You're lucky being in Washington over the summer. Just think of all that information right there in the Library of Congress."

"Guess you're right. Isn't that terrible news about Sister Calista? She's so young to have anything like cancer."

"It may not be. Remember what she said; it could be just to rule out something serious. Besides, she is such a healthy-looking person, and x-rays have been proven wrong before."

"I hope so, I think she's one of the best teachers up here and has made the debating club a lot of fun." The girls headed for the parking lot in silence.

A week after the surgery, there was a message in Sister Calista's mailbox to contact her doctor. When Sister Calista had called his office, an appointment was made for the following day.

"Sit down, Sister." She didn't like the ominous sound in his voice. "I'm afraid I have some bad news as far as the results of the biopsy."

"Is it cancer?"

"No, you have a disease called pulmonary fibrosis, which severely scars the lungs. The cause is unknown, but the illness gets progressively worse."

"But you said the scar tissue had been from pleurisy," pleading to erase the words she had just heard.

"It could have been from pleurisy—that's why I wanted the biopsy, to rule out this disease, I didn't mention it to you at the time because I didn't want to alarm you unnecessarily."

"Is there a cure?" By now her hands started to sweat and she felt faint. The doctor asked her if she would like to lie down. "No, I'll be all right. I just have to sit here awhile."

"There is no known cure, other than a lung transplant; of course I will put you on the waiting list immediately."

"Is it that serious?" She couldn't stop the tears now, the doctor's words had registered: *no known cure*. "But I feel so good—how could this be?"

"The antibiotics worked for the short term. You'll have recurrences with coughing. I'll give you some cardiopulmonary exercises to build your strength." The doctor's words ran into each other: *For the short term, recurrences with coughing*. "It's all a bad dream, this cannot be, I'm too young to die."

"I'll have the nurse bring you a glass of water."

"How long will I have before—" She never got to finish the sentence.

"Four to six months, perhaps longer with the cardiopulmonary exercises."

"What are my chances of getting a lung transplant?"

"That is difficult to say; sometimes a relative can be found who is willing to donate and the match is good, or you stay on the waiting list until one becomes available. Do you have any living relatives?"

"A brother…I have a brother who is a priest and…" She had almost said "a daughter" but stopped short.

"You may want to talk it over with him. Right now I'd like to give you this instruction booklet on the exercises." By now she had composed herself and the doctor's words were registering in her brain. "I'll want to see you every two weeks from now on. My receptionist will set up the appointments. I only wish I had been able to give you some better news."

Sister Calista closed the door to the doctor's office and quickly headed for the elevator. She fought back the tears and had been glad there wasn't anyone in the hallway. *How can this be?* The question rolled around and around like a spinning top. *I feel fine—how can I really be dying with only four months to live?* The elevator door sliced open, and she quickly entered. One woman, who smiled and moved over to let her in, had been the only other occupant. The haunting question hammered inside her mind all the way home as she drove home weaving in and out of the busy traffic.

"Sure, I can come up for Memorial Day." The sound of her brother's voice felt good. "I'll pick you up and we can drive up to Cape Cod. Can you arrange to stay a few days?"

"I'm pretty sure I can." She had called him immediately. The sound of his voice had been the reassurance she needed. "Will you call ahead to make arrangements or shall I?"

"You can do it. Make it for two days after the holiday. This will give us time to explore Providencetown."

"I can't wait to see you." She stopped short. She couldn't blurt this over the phone. "I'll let you know as soon as I firm up the reservations."

"Is there anything wrong? You sound upset."

"Nothing that won't keep until I see you." They continued to talk about the upcoming mini vacation and set a date for him to pick her up.

The spring weather did not reflect Sister Calista's ordeal, nor did smells of the azaleas, ablaze in all different colors, that dotted the walks of all the quads leading to dormitories, classrooms, and administration buildings. Chattering students' voices could be heard as they gathered in clusters and sat anywhere like flowers at will with the advent of warm weather.

Sister Calista inhaled the perfume of a bed of pink azaleas as she walked past the administration building headed for her last debating class of the term. *What am I going to tell these students?* She thought to herself. *I can't have these girls upset all summer about my medical condition, but I certainly don't want to minimize the seriousness. After all, I may not be here when they return in September.* She shuddered at the thought.

"Girls, girls, please take your seats this won't take long, I just want to make sure everyone has an assignment." The students filed into the rows of desk seats and she continued. "This debate is an important one, and if everyone researches her given material, I'm sure we'll have a great chance of walking away with first prize, so girls, do your homework carefully and have a wonderful summer vacation. As for me I'm going to start mine off with a trip to Cape Cod with my brother, Tim, a place I always wanted to visit. That's about it. See you in September, God willing."

No one asked about her test results. She wouldn't have to deal with it—so she thought.

"Sister," Bridget had stayed behind after all the girls left the room. "How did your test results pan out? You didn't mention it during class."

"Not too well." She didn't want to lie to her, but she couldn't bring herself to tell the whole truth. "It seems I have a lung disease—nothing contagious; it's something I have always had. I have to do some breathing exercises to strengthen my lungs."

"That's horrible. Isn't there an operation or medication you can take to cure it?"

"I'm afraid not, Bridget. I could have a lung transplant, but that's down the road a bit."

"A lung transplant, oh Sister." Tears welled up in Bridget's eyes and she automatically hugged her. The closeness of her child's body, in spite of her devastating sickness, made her smile.

"Now, now Bridget, where is your faith?" she said, consoling the weeping girl.

"It just doesn't seem fair."

"God works in strange ways. Who are we to question?" She gathered strength in her own words as she held on to her daughter and wiped away her tears. How often she had wanted to reach out and just touch her child, but it had taken this turn of events to make it a reality.

"I'm sorry, Sister. I hope I didn't upset you." Bridget sensed her gentle release and stood back.

"No, you haven't upset me. What does upset me is how to break this news to my brother, Tim."

"He doesn't know yet? You said you were going away on vacation, Cape Cod." Bridget's voice trailed off.

"Yes, but I couldn't tell him over the phone. Somewhere between here and Massachusetts I must tell him. It's only going to ruin the vacation. Maybe I'll wait until the return trip home."

"Whatever you decide, I'm sure you will know the right time. It's just that you look so…so healthy. It's so hard to believe!"

"That's what I keep telling myself, but I did see the x-rays and the biopsy confirmed the diagnosis."

Bridget headed for the door, turned, and tearfully said good-bye again.

"Remember, you have the viability angle on the debate," Sister Callista said. "I'm counting on you for any new medical news on that issue. Keep focused and see you in September, God willing."

Chapter Eight

"Propriety would have been a better word than privacy, don't you think?" Julia started to fluff the cushions on the settee and placed them upright next to the wicker chair where Clifford had been sitting. Her words had been meant for her husband when he had commented on his daughter Bridget's remarks.

"Moth-er," Bridget said, dragging the word out, "we know how adamant you are about this issue. Try and remember this is a debate."

Bridget had invited her friend Patricia to spend time with her before she left for Washington. They had planned to work on the upcoming debate, discussing the type of research they planned to use. The girls had spent the day at the beach, and after supper, they,, along with Julia and Clifford, retired to the screened porch and the conversation centered on the upcoming November debate.

"Patricia has the angle on the right to privacy, and I have to research medical documents to see when viability in a fetus occurs," Bridget responded to her father's question about their assignments.

"I'm in agreement with the right to privacy when it comes to this abortion debate," said her father. "But as far as viability, I'm completely in the dark."

"Why wouldn't you be?" said Julia. "You're a man."

At that, Clifford had gotten up and retreated into the kitchen.

"Mom, why can't we have a discussion about this without personal attacks? Dad may not be able to share your view, but I don't hear him verbally abusing you when you make your position as a right-to-life advocate. It's not the first time I've heard you strike out at him. After all, he's not the United States Supreme Court. He didn't make abortion on demand the law of the land." *No*, thought Julia, *but he did make a demand many years ago.* For years recurring nightmares about the horrible night in Maryland had haunted Julia, and now the nightmares had started again almost at the same time Bridget came home from school announcing her coming participation in a debate on abortion.

"I'm sorry, dear." And with those words she too disappeared into the kitchen leaving the girls alone on the porch.

"Your mother makes no bones about her position on right to life," Patricia said. "But my mother is the same way. It must be the strong influence of their Catholic upbringing. To tell you the truth, I don't believe most women realize how archaic some of these laws were."

"You're right about that. Remember the story Sister Calista told us about her brother Tim's lawyer friend and how some doctors were held on criminal charges for treating women who had been experiencing a normal abortion. If those laws had been addressed years ago, we wouldn't be facing this debate in November."

"OK, Mr. Daniel Webster," said Bridget, trying to take the edge off what had been an enjoyable day until her mother's snide remarks. "Let's compare notes." The girls shared notes on what they had accomplished to date and worked for another hour before retiring.

"Good morning," Julia greeted her husband. She had wanted to apologize last night in the kitchen, but Clifford had already gone to bed. He ignored her greeting and headed for the back door. "Aren't you going to have any breakfast?"

"I didn't think you would want to eat with someone as insensitive as me. I suppose you will never forgive me for what happened years ago, and I don't know how much more I can take of your nasty digs."

"I'm sorry, Cliff, it's just that I've been having those recurring nightmares again, and they frighten me. Ever since Bridget came home. It must be that assignment she is working on. I'm truly sorry. It was uncalled for and I apologize. It seems the hurtful words spill out from my mouth before my brain kicks in. It's the strangest thing."

"Well," he turned, "I could use a cup of coffee." Julia reached up for the coffee pot and poured a cup for her husband. "Maybe you should see a doctor about the nightmares."

"Whatever could he do? I'm not about to tell him about something I did years ago and have regretted ever since. No, I'm sure they'll subside."

"Suit yourself." He landed a peck on her cheek and was gone.

The trip up the east coast to Massachusetts had been a leisurely one. Sister Calista and Tim stopped at a retreat house in Connecticut.

"Let's not do any night driving," said Tim when he picked her up at the school. "I've made reservations to stay overnight at St. Thomas More's."

"Fine by me. I have nothing pressing to drag me back."

She thought of her last moments with Bridget and realized that at some time during this trip, she would have to tell her brother about her illness.

Holding back from him had been difficult. Since Bridget's arrival at school, her happiness had been perfect. Seeing Bridget around the campus grounds, watching her mingle with other students, gave her complete joy. She had been tempted a few times to share her long-kept secret with him, but this sudden turn of events prohibited it. He wouldn't hesitate to save her life even if it meant upsetting other people. She knew her brother.

It had happened without warning. She started to cough, first intermittently, then uncontrollably.

"Are you all right? Do you want me to drive for a while and give you a break? I thought you had gone to the doctor's and gotten rid of that cough."

They had just entered the parkway after leaving the retreat house in Mystic, Connecticut. Traffic had been light so she had little trouble maneuvering to the shoulder of the road and coming to a stop. Tim stared in dismay while she doubled up over the steering wheel, continuing to cough.

"Reach into my pocketbook and give me that spray." Tim leaned over the front seat, searched her handbag, and retrieved the spray bottle. Once she inhaled the vapors from the bottle, she stopped hacking.

He sat next to his sister, startled at the suddenness of the event. As he looked at her, surprise still registered on his face. She couldn't help but break down into tears.

"Now, now," he comforted her, his arm around her shoulder. "It's passed."

"For now," she said between sobs, burying her head into his chest.

"Whatever do you mean, Una?" The sound of her childhood name made her dig even deeper into his chest, as if by doing so it would erase all that she had yet to tell him.

"My cough is not something that is going to get better." She spoke in halting phrases between her sobs. "My doctor tells me I have some kind of lung disease—"

"Lung disease, TB, that's not something—" He interrupted her, not letting her finish.

"No, not TB. It has a medical name…I can't think of it right now." She started to gain control and pulled back from him. "At first the doctor thought it was nothing more than scar tissue on my lungs from pleurisy."

"Pleurisy? When did you ever have pleurisy?" Tim's face screwed up in disbelief.

"Right, that's what I thought when he told me, but evidently one can have pleurisy and think it's just a bad cough. When the cough subsides, the lungs show scars of the infection in an x-ray. When he looked at my x-rays, he told me that's what he thought they were. He didn't want to say much more until he took a biopsy, so that's why I never mentioned any of this to you until now. The results came back and showed I have this life-threatening lung disease and," at this point she threw her arms around her brother's neck. "Unless I get a lung transplant I don't have much to look forward to."

Her brother, still registering shock on his face, hugged his sister, and he too began to cry. "How can this be…you're so young?" His voice trailed off, and they both sat there a long time. "When can I see this doctor to find out about the compatibility of my lung?" Tim released his grip, having gotten control of his emotions.

"I'm not at that stage yet. I have these exercises I have to do, and the medication helps somewhat. It's only when I cough so unexpectedly, like now, that it really alarms me. I get scared when I can't catch my breath. It's an awful feeling," she said, still visibly shaken.

"Who wouldn't be? Not being able to breathe would frighten anyone. You would think he would have recommended the transplant immediately."

"That's another thing. There's a waiting list for these things. He's put me on it, and of course, he asked about relatives." Her eyes filled with tears as she looked at her brother, who, up until an hour ago, had been laughing and telling her corny jokes. "I feel terrible ruining our vacation this way. I knew I had to tell you. I was going to tell you about it on the way home, but then this happened."

"Don't be ridiculous—there never would have been a right moment to let me know. I'm only sorry I didn't know sooner so you wouldn't have had to carry this weight all by yourself." With this, he hugged her again.

Her brother's nearness, his strong grip, made her feel secure and safe as if nothing could harm her, not even this terrible disease. They talked about getting in touch with her doctor as soon as they got back from vacation, and gradually she managed to smile up at him and tell him she was relieved that he finally knew.

"Let me drive from now on; you can be my co-pilot." He gave her the map he had been studying.

Tim drove, not talking much, but thinking about what had just happened. *What if my lung isn't compatible? How can I tell her I know about her having a child years ago? Mom told me that in the strictest of confidence and I promised her I would never let Una know that I knew. If my lung doesn't match up, can I break my silence about the child who possibly could save her life? How could we find her? Where would we start looking?*

Maybe I can keep my promise. There's the other secret of Mom's: Maura McHugh. I was never asked to keep silent about her.

"I'm so sorry to have ruined our vacation," Sister Calista put down the map, turned, and looked out her window.

"You didn't ruin anything. It's just that I've been thinking about the lung transplant and hoping that mine is compatible."

"Right." He mustered a smile and reached over, patting her on the back. "Cape Cod, here we come."

She leaned back, stretched out her legs, closed her eyes, and tried to sleep, but her thoughts kept her from that.

What would I have ever done without him? Ever since they were children, he had been her hero. Like the time Charley Gallagher's coat caught fire as they marched around a bonfire in the lots of Intervale Avenue.

It had been a day of sledding during the winter months, and as usual, the children had been performing their ritual of encircling it to keep warm while waiting for the "mickeys" to cook on the fire. Charley had gotten too close and his coat flamed up and he began to run. Without thinking, Tim chased after him and wrestled him to the ground, using his own body to put out the flames. Luckily, neither of them were seriously burned. Charley had one of his older brother's jackets on, and because the sleeves were much too long he had to roll them up, the thickness of the material had saved him. Tim, when he wrestled him to the ground, had the good sense to use his back as the smothering agent, so his burns were only in that area.

Memories of Tim's Herculean courage of long ago filled her mind for the moment, enabling her to finally doze off as Tim drove.

Chapter Nine

Julia stayed behind after mass until everyone had left the church. When she poked her head into the sacristy, Monsignor Gore had just taken off the last of his vestments.

"Julia, how are you? How is Clifford?"

"Can I talk to you a minute? I have a favor to ask."

"Surely, come in." The altar boys had left, and the two of them were alone.

"Do you remember if my mom ever had the house blessed?"

The monsignor looked at Julia surprised. "I couldn't say for sure. Your mom and dad lived in your house long before I came here, so there is a possibility someone else could have done it, but if you'd like, I could do it for you again." Ever since Bridget had left for Washington, Julia had been plagued with the nightmares. It had gotten so bad she hated to go to bed at night and had begun watching late night movies and talk shows. She had begun to think some of the characters on the screen were giving her messages. She knew something was radically wrong and believed that the devil had invaded her home. Clifford had commented on her new habits but suspected nothing about her mental condition.

At times Julia had no control over her compulsive actions. Once she found herself waking up in the middle of the night, going downstairs to the kitchen and emptying out one of the drawers that contained odds and ends. She would gather together things, like half boxes of birthday candles, corkscrews, pieces of string, and place them outside on the porch. While she was doing this, she would think how strange it was, but she couldn't stop. Another time she rose early in the morning and rinsed a pair of her panties in the sink placing them outside on the back porch. She thought these actions odd, even smiling while she completed the task. "I can't believe I'm doing this," she would say to herself. It wasn't till one hot night in July that her actions caught Cliff's attention.

Julia had started sleeping in the guest room, and Clifford thought it was because she didn't like the air conditioner on all night. When Clifford was awakened by a voice coming from the guest room, he bolted up in his bed, went into the hall, and opened the guest room door. There he saw his wife clutching a crucifix to her chest, pacing back and forth while mumbling something about God not forsaking her. When he approached, she threw the cross on the bed and ran screaming into the bathroom, locking the door behind her. For hours Clifford begged her intermittently to open it. When she finally did come out, he tried to calm her. She was exhausted and he held her close to him, gently rocking her. He realized she needed help and decided to take her to the hospital himself rather than call 911.

Clifford sat her on the edge of the bed, all the while whispering to her that they were going to a place where she would get better, and she agreed, shaking her head. He raced into their bedroom, reached into her closet, and grabbed at the first dress and pair of shoes his hands touched. Gently, he pulled the dress over her head, coaxing her to stand for the minute and then sitting her back down again. He then slipped on a pair of her sandals. On the way to the hospital, her compulsive behavior returned and she rolled down her window and thrust her hand out, mumbling inaudible commands at imaginary people. He pressed hard on the accelerator.

At the hospital, Clifford was directed to mental health admittance. Julia was asked to sign herself in. When given a pen by the Chinese doctor, she balked at signing her name in ink, so they agreed to her signature in pencil. After her admittance, the doctor immediately gave her a shot. Julia was then put in a room with a mattress on the floor and no other furniture. She was given a hospital gown and a nurse removed her clothing. Exhausted, she lay on the mattress, and in a matter of minutes fell into a deep sleep.

When she woke she was frightened and shocked by the four stark white walls and the mattress without a bed frame that she was lying on. She remembered the night before, Clifford dressing her at home, her uncontrollable actions she no longer could hide from him, the car ride to the hospital, the refusing to sign her name in ink. It seemed so long ago, but whatever medication she received combined with the night's sleep brought her back to normalcy. She wanted to scream; her sparse hospital surroundings suggested treatment for violent patients who would harm themselves. She had no such thoughts. Julia rose from the mattress on the floor. She could hear footsteps of people walking outside the only door in the room and walked over to the door, stood on tiptoe, and gently tapped on the encased window almost out of her reach. An attendant came to the door and unlocked her nocturnal cell.

She asked Julia if she would like to get dressed. Julia walked down a hall that resembled the deck of a cruise ship; only the people shuffling by quickly dispelled that idea. When she finally arrived at the room assigned by the nurse, she noticed a woman lying in one of the beds. The woman's face was turned toward the wall, and she never moved. Julia's clothes were laid out on her bed and she quickly dressed herself. She asked the woman facing the wall if she had been in the hospital long, but the woman said nothing. Julia continued to dress and try to make conversation, asking the woman if she had been married and did she have children.

Finally the woman turned. "I'm not married, and I don't have any children," she bellowed while two bony hands fingered the blanket.

Julia, shocked by the appearance of the woman, wished she had never spoken. Her thinning white hair sparsely covered her entire head. Sunken cavernous dark eyes in an elongated wrinkled face glared at Julia. She recoiled into a corner of the room and her roommate pulled the blanket over her head and turned her body to the wall. *Clifford where are you?* she thought.

The nurse came in and Julia asked if she could get something to eat. The nurse said there was a cafeteria down the hall and that the doctor would be in soon to see her. Julia was famished and headed down to the cafeteria. She couldn't resist smiling to herself when she lifted the cover on her dish. Piled high on her plate was Chinese food. She thought to herself, *Chinese admitting doctor, Chinese food. I hope I'm still in New Jersey.*

As she returned to her room, her doctor appeared. She asked how she felt and appeared amazed at Julia's quick recovery from the night before. Julia didn't volunteer just how frightened she had been, and the doctor said she would be going home but to be sure and have the prescription filled and take it all. Julia promised that she would and was told her husband was outside and as soon as the doctor left he came into the room.

"Let's get out of here," Julia said, walking toward her husband. Cliff looked at her in amazement and couldn't believe the transformation in his wife from the night before.

"How do you feel? Are you all right?" His questions annoyed Julia because no, she wasn't all right—she was scared and she didn't feel much like discussing it with him.

"Yes, let's just get out of here." She quickened her pace in the corridor, making her way toward the elevator.

"Did the doctor suggest any follow-up therapy?"

"No, she told me to have this prescription filled and make sure to take all the pills."

"I can drop it off on the way home." Julia handed him the prescription.

In the days that followed Clifford didn't stay late at the paper. He had been upset and worried since that night in the hospital. Julia had asked him not to say anything to Bridget, and he said he wouldn't but had reservations about that promise. His wife took umbrage if he started to question her about the things that had led up to that eventful night, and Julia snapped at him for the least little thing.

"Don't tell me you're going to have another martini." Julia looked up from the book she had been reading.

"As a matter of fact I am." Annoyed at her tone, he intended to leave his empty cocktail glass on the table, but the silences they shared since her return from the hospital had slipped into his having several drinks before and after dinner. The conversation about his work and her daily routine that had been shared for years disappeared. Julia had crying bouts during the day that she would not tell her husband about; she had been afraid of what he might suggest.

"What's wrong with us? Why can't we talk about this?" Clifford's words slurred after sitting back in the chair with his drink.

"Wrong, you ask what's wrong? I'll tell you what's wrong. I'm sick and tired of watching you get sloshed every night. Ever since I came home from the hospital I feel as if you're constantly watching me, like I'm going to go off the deep end again, and then to top it off there's no conversation and you proceed to quietly get drunk."

"What's wrong with having a few drinks and unwinding?" He snapped back at her, "And as far as conversation goes, any time I speak you take my head off." His words stung. She had been right about him watching her. He couldn't help it. Fear gripped him at the paper, as he thought about her at home alone, and he changed his routine of staying late and supervising last-minute details about getting the paper out. He handed that job down to Les, his managing editor. Julia realized her husband's change in his routine and resented it. Clifford's fear manifested in playing warden to his wife and she sensed it.

The morning after this angry verbal exchange Julia awoke to find Clifford gone for the office. She started to cry softly in her bed and then thought to herself, *This is ridiculous. I can't go on living like this.* She went downstairs, rummaged around for the telephone book, found it, and looked under mental health for a marriage counseling psychologist.

Bridget loved the excitement generated by her new job in Senator Lautenberg's office and quickly learned the daily routine. She was complimented on her quick study of what had been expected of her. There hadn't been to much time for socializing outside business hours because of her research on the debate. Weekends had been spent in the library looking up medical records, state court decisions on abortion issues, and the like. Patricia's phone call saying she was coming down for a visit had been welcome news to Bridget. There had been a Georgia O'Keeffe exhibition at one of the local museums, and when Bridget told Patricia about it they arranged for a mini weekend from work. Both girls enjoyed O'Keeffe's paintings, in fact Bridget liked them so much she wrote a poem about the famous artist.

The guide at the museum waved her hands to the throng of people milling around the entrance to the O'Keeffe exhibition as if she had been gathering chicks. Bridget and Patricia complied with the hand motions to follow.

"This is a plus; we're going to get some bio on her life as well as seeing her marvelous paintings," Patricia said.

"I didn't think we would have a tour guide. I've often wondered how she hooked up with Stieglitz, him being so much older than she." The two girls followed the crowd and listened to the comments made on O'Keeffe's life.

What interested both girls very much had been O'Keeffe's early charcoal drawings made while O'Keeffe had been teaching and involved with another professor at the same college. A man, by the name of McMahon, caught her eye before she ever became involved with the famous photographer Alfred Stieglitz.

"Is it me, or do you see some of the things I see in those abstract drawings she made while in that emotional state after McMahon's Thanksgiving visit?" Bridget said out loud while the two girls, who by now had left the group, sat on a stone bench to study the charcoal sketches.

"They do look like sonograms of a fetus," Patricia said.

"If the guide hadn't quoted what O'Keeffe had written to her friend Anita Politnzer about how she felt before she sketched those drawings, I don't think I could have made the association, or maybe it's because I'm knee deep in research about when conception takes place."

"Could be," laughed Patricia. "Maybe that's why Stieglitz's famous quote, 'Finally, a woman on paper' makes sense to the art world. She may have wanted to—or in fact had sex with McMahon over that weekend and when she wrote to her friend about having something she wanted to say, as a painter she described it best by showing the beginnings of birth on canvas…almost like a writer puts words on paper. Maybe you can use this in your presentation about how some woman feel when they realize or even think about being pregnant. It's just a thought."

"You're right, even O'Keeffe's biographer, Roxanna Robinson thought as much. I jotted down her exact words in my notebook…" Bridget reached into her backpack and flipped through pages and then started to read aloud. *"Movement is portrayed by ripples suggesting the liquid surge of flowing water—a fluid, peaceful form of natural power*. Stieglitz discovered O'Keeffe's talent for expressing female emotions on canvas, but her female biographer, knowing what was going on at that point in her life, paints us another picture. Don't you think?"

"Could be, who knows, she could have even been pregnant and had an abortion." Patricia rose from the bench. "I'm famished. Know of any good Italian restaurants? I'd love a plate of pasta."

"Not really, but we could ask at the front desk on our way out." The two girls headed for the entrance, laughing and talking as they made their way.

Chapter Ten

"It's not going to hit us," Julia said, holding the door opened for Clifford to carry in the wicker furniture from the screened-in porch. "The news bulletin said Connecticut will be where it will hit land."

"That's a relief, but I think I'll feel better knowing this stuff won't be blown all around out here." News bulletins had been warning of Adrian, the first hurricane of the season heading toward the Jersey shoreline all morning long, and Clifford had risen early to secure the outside furniture from being damaged.

It had been two weeks since Julia's first visit to the psychologist, and she noticed a marked improvement. The nightmares had stopped altogether, and she found herself sleeping through the night. She had also gone back to her own bedroom after Clifford said he would raise the temperature setting on the air conditioner so it wouldn't turn on and off as much.

"Maybe the rain will cool things off a bit. I'm glad we're not getting the brunt of the storm, but the rain will be a welcome relief from all this heat we've been having." Julia was scheduled for a visit to the psychologist that afternoon, but the threat of the storm made her think about canceling the appointment.

"I have to get down to the paper as soon as I get this furniture all squared away. Will you be all right? You mentioned something about an appointment this afternoon; maybe you had better cancel it. You wouldn't want to get caught up in heavy winds and rains if it's not important." Clifford had noticed the change in Julia's behavior as well. Since the night of the martini incident, she had seemed more in control of her actions. Things began to seem normal again, and he resumed his long working days.

"I'll get it," Clifford said as he wiggled his way between the furniture he had been arranging in the sun parlor to get to the phone. "Hello, yes, just a minute. It's Dr. Lovett's office for you Julia."

Julia picked up the extension in the kitchen. "Yes, that will be fine, next Monday at ten." She turned and found Clifford staring at her.

"Who is Dr. Lovett? Is there something wrong? You hadn't mentioned you were seeing a doctor." Her husband's machine-gun-fashion questions rattled her.

"He's a psychologist."

"A psychologist? You told me the doctor had not mentioned any follow-up therapy."

"She did."

"Why didn't you tell me?"

"I was going to…in time…when I was ready."

"Well, I'm glad you're going. When did you start?"

"Remember the night I chewed you out about the martini? That was it. The next day I made an appointment and have been going weekly. I feel so much better. He really has helped me understand myself better and how to cope with my problems."

"I wondered what kind of miracle had taken place." He gathered up his wife in his arms kissed her long and passionately.

"It's good to have us back in sync."

Julia nestled against his chest. "Stay home," she whispered in his ear. He lifted her up and carried her upstairs to their bedroom.

The rain started. Sister struggled to open the compact umbrella she had brought with her after looking out her window and noticing the darkening sky. Normally, in August, the campus grounds showed little activity. But a Writers' Conference had been scheduled that week, and clusters of women darted in and around the buildings. Finally, the umbrella went up. The rain was sending people running for shelter; the administration building was lined with women with drenched hair. Sister weaved her way through the sound of their laughter and gained entrance to the main office.

"Any mail for Sister Calista?" She asked the student at the front desk.

"I'll look and see, Sister. Yes, there is something for you," she said and handed her a letter.

Sister looked at the envelope that bore Bridget's return address in Washington. Excitedly, she ripped open the envelope. The letter was cordial and inquired about her health and explained how she had adapted to the line of work in the senator's office. She also spoke of Patricia's visit and their trip to the museum and how they both had feelings about O'Keeffe's paintings looking like modern-day sonograms. *Interesting*, thought Sister about the sketches. She didn't know much about O'Keeffe or any of her work, so her curiosity became aroused.

What a thoughtful person she is, to write and ask about me. It had been the only inquiry she had received from any of her students about her health, and the fact it had been Bridget made it all the more special. *I'll have to get to the library and see if I can get any information on O'Keeffe before I answer her letter.* She passed through the glass door to find the rain-drenched women making decisions about making a run for the dorms. By now the wind had picked up, rain splattered across her face and when she opened the umbrella, it blew inside out. She ran across the quadrant, trying to right the umbrella but to no avail. The library was a distance for her to make a dash. She suddenly felt faint and everything went black.

"Whatever made you go out in a hurricane?" She recognized her brother Tim's voice. He was sitting in a chair next to her bed.

"Where am I?" She looked down at the intravenous inserted in the back of her hand.

"New Rochelle General Hospital. Some students saw you pass out when you were running on campus. Where were you headed anyway in that rain?"

"It didn't look that bad when I decided to see if I had any mail. In fact it wasn't even raining when I first went out. It just came up all of a sudden. I guess when I started to run that's the last thing I remember. I was headed for the library to look up something and then nothing."

"The doctor said you should stay in bed for a few days to regain strength."

"Do I have to stay in the hospital, or can I do this at home?"

"He said he wanted to keep you overnight, but I told him I knew as soon as you came around you would want out of here, so I told him I would see to it that you would stay in bed. I'm going to be your jailer for a few days."

"You're a sweetheart." She tried to raise herself to hug him with her free arm. He didn't like the way she looked. She had lost weight and was very pale looking.

"Oh, by the way, I've been in touch with your doctor and have set up an appointment for the compatibility test." He purposely left out the word *lung*. "September fifteenth was the closest he could get for me." He turned and found the doctor checking the chart at the foot of the bed.

"How are you feeling? I've been in touch with your doctor, and he advises bed rest for you. Your brother here has promised to see you get it so when that IV is done you're free to go home."

"Do you know what they did with my clothes?" Sister Calista asked.

"I'll send the nurse in; she should be able to tell you more about that."

"I should have thought about stopping at your place and getting fresh clothes, but when I got the call, I just rushed right to the hospital and never thought about it."

"That's OK; I'm sure they're dry by now."

The nurse came in and removed the IV and brought in her clothes.

On the trip home Sister asked Tim if he would do her a favor and get as much information as he could on the painter O'Keeffe. She knew he would not let her get out of bed for a day or so. This would be a perfect time to learn something about this famous woman painter.

After settling his sister in her apartment, he took off to the campus library. The hurricane-like weather had passed, and he found it pleasant strolling up the library steps. He engaged the help of a librarian and she weighted him down with not only letters of O'Keeffe that had been compiled in numerous books but also picture books of her very famous paintings in addition to a biography.

When he returned to his sister's apartment, she couldn't help but laugh at the sight of him trying to balance all he had in his possession.

"There, that should keep you busy for a day or two. Why the sudden interest in O'Keeffe?"

"One of my students, Bridget Clark, mentioned her in a letter and I want to check out her findings."

"Promise me you'll stay put. I'd like to check back at my motel to see if there are any messages, shower, and get squared away."

"Promise, you go ahead. I'll be fine."

He leaned over and kissed his sister on the cheek.

Sister spread the volumes of reading material on her bed. Where to start? She picked up one of the coffee-table-type books containing reproductions of O'Keeffe's work. *They certainly are beautiful*, she thought to herself laying the book down and picking up another volume containing letters written by O'Keeffe to her friends and art critics. For hours she poured over the plethora of information at her disposal.

Several hours after reading personal letters of O'Keeffe and studying her paintings, she couldn't help but think O'Keeffe's emotional state had something to do with the etchings on her abstract charcoal drawings. According to a letter to a close friend, the drawings came about after a visit from a man whom she was involved with. *Hmm*, she wondered if O'Keeffe's feelings for an intimate relationship with the man could have been transferred into the abstract drawings, much like one would write a love letter. Sister Calista noted her thoughts on the pad where she was jotting down notes on her findings. Painters sometimes paint chiaroscuro. Her early charcoal sketches made her future husband and art critic exclaim, "Finally, a woman on paper." He, too, could have seen the third dimension.

She heard the front door open. "It's only me," her brother called. "Why don't you turn on a light in here?" He flicked on the lamp next to her bed.

"I didn't notice it getting dark. I got so involved with these books. When my student mentioned how some of her abstract drawings reminded her of sonograms, I couldn't wait to see what she was talking about."

"Let me see," said Tim. He reached over and picked up one of the volumes. "She certainly did paint large, not exactly to my taste. I like quiet scenes."

"Her paintings vary. In her early days, she concentrated on flowers, still life, and the like, and then when she moved out West she got involved with animal bones."

"I can see," laughed her brother, holding up one of the books depicting a cow's skull with a flower in the eye socket.

"Would you believe after O'Keeffe came back from New Mexico and had an exhibition of these paintings many art critics wrote that she had a religious epiphany while out West that inspired her work."

"You're kidding," her brother said as he kept looking at the book in his lap. "I suppose art is of a personal nature. Oh well," He laid the book back on her bed. "Now that you have worked all afternoon, how about some dinner? I stopped at the stores and picked up some steaks."

"Sounds good to me." Sister swung her legs to the side of the bed, attempting to get out. "I'd like to shower and get dressed while you're playing cook in the kitchen."

"That was delicious; I didn't realize how hungry I was," Sister Calista said. By now the two of them had settled in Sister's small living room after cleaning up the dinner things and stacking all the books of O'Keeffe on her living room floor. "I certainly got a lot done today, and I think I can use some of the information in helping my team sum up their closing arguments for the debate."

"Do you want me to return these books tomorrow? I'll stop by before I head back home."

"No, I want to read some more of the letters. O'Keeffe wasn't much for writing, and the few she did write were not lengthy. I can bring them back a few at a time. I have a couple of weeks; thanks anyway." They talked for an hour or so and she promised her brother she would rest another day before starting back to her schedule. They said their good-byes and Tim left for the motel.

Senator Lautenberg's office gave notice that the office would be closed on Friday of Labor Day weekend and that all interns were free to go home for good. Congressman James Hughes of Spring Lake died suddenly. Senator Lautenberg planned to attend the funeral.

Bridget welcomed the early closing because originally she was told the job would last for a week after the holiday. She enjoyed Washington, even had some interesting young men on staff with whom she had dinner with a few times. The two months flew by and she believed she gained experience that would be beneficial to her both in her studies and future career choice.

Her parents were glad to hear she was going to be home for awhile before going back to school.

"That's wonderful," her mother said after Bridget called and told about the early dismissal. "The weather has been beautiful after the first hurricane of the season, so you can get some beach time in before going back to school. It's too bad about Congressman James Hughes. He and your father were classmates at St. Bonaventure. Your father wanted to attend the funeral, but because of the crowd from the House of Representatives and Senate, it will be by invitation only. His widow asked our choir to sing, so I get to go."

"It was an unexpected death, wasn't it?"

"Yes," Julia said. "He suffered a massive heart attack, no warning, just hit him all of a sudden."

"Senator Lautenberg had nothing to say but what a great legislator he had been and he would be sorely missed."

"I'm not surprised; your father said as much, too. Anyway, let me know when you're headed home so I can expect you."

"Great, maybe I'll call Patricia and have her stay for awhile. Would you mind?"

"Not at all. It's going to feel good to have you at home, and no, not at all, invite her."

"I'll call and ask her; thanks Mom."

The drive home from Washington took longer than Bridget thought. She ran into construction around Delaware, and to make matters worse, there was a high-speed chase that ended up with two or three cars piled on top of each other near the construction site that brought the normal flow of traffic to a snail's pace and finally to a complete standstill for an hour while police cars, ambulances, and fire trucks converged on the scene. Bits and pieces of conversation from law enforcement at the carnage said some kids had stolen a car and, when stopped by a police officer for speeding, took off when they couldn't produce the ownership. The bent and twisted cars piled on top of each other while help tried to ply the victims from the rubble sent shivers down Bridget's spine and she couldn't wait to get away from such a dreadful scene.

The sight of her home when she pulled into her driveway made her feel safe and secure. She rushed up the front steps and tore open the screen door. "Anyone home?" her voice echoed throughout. Her mother appeared on the landing and rushed down.

"You're home, sweetheart."

Bridget ran to greet her and gave her a bear hug greeting.

"It's good to be home. I thought I'd never get here. There was a terrible accident around Delaware, and it took forever before the police could move the cars. It was just awful, but I'm home. Have you anything cold to drink? I'm dying of thirst."

"Of course, come into the kitchen. I'll fix you a bite to eat, too."

They were just finishing up eating when Bridget's father entered the kitchen. "I thought I heard a familiar voice in here." Bridget rushed to greet her dad and give him a hug and kiss.

"She had a nightmare of a drive home," said Julia. "I'm so glad you're safe and sound. Did you get a chance to call Patricia?"

"Yes, and she will be here tomorrow. Right now I'd like to take a quick shower and head for the beach."

"Go right ahead," said her mother. Bridget hugged her dad again and raced up the stairs.

"How was the funeral?" Clifford asked.

"I never saw so many politicians in one place at the same time. I caught myself hanging over the choir balcony checking on senators like Kennedy, Bradley, and Lautenberg. It felt like attending a move premiere. At one point I made a mental note to remind myself why I was there, and you know, the weirdest thing happened to me while I headed down the aisle to approach the communion rail."

"What was that?"

"The line moved ever so slowly because of the vast crowds; just before I reached the communion rail I felt this…this energy. It was the strangest feeling. I looked over at the filled pews and thought there were millions of people being represented here by these legislators. This is probably why. It felt really weird."

"Not really, things like that happen. I remember being at a meeting with newspaper publishers in New York when Forbes of the Fortune Five Hundred entered the room. I could feel a strong sense of energy as he circulated the room."

"I'm glad to hear that; at least I don't feel I'm not the only one who has had such an experience.

"Is this a picture of your grandmother?" Sister Calista asked. Pictures were strewn about her bed. As she went to sit, Sister happened to pick up one of Bridget and her grandmother on the boardwalk.

"Yes, that had been taken just before she passed away. She lived with us after my grandfather died. My parents thought it would be best if all of us lived in her house since she didn't want to move and the house was really too much for her to manage by herself. I loved her very much and miss her."

Sister Calista placed the picture on the student desk along with several others and sat on the bed.

"I have been reading a great deal about O'Keeffe since you wrote to me and I believe I have a great argument for summation. I didn't mean to pounce on you so quickly. Any news when Patricia is due back?"

"Some time tomorrow. She spent Labor Day weekend at my home, and we went over our notes so we're ready to put them together whenever class starts up next week."

"Good, I'll see if I can round up the rest of the team. I have to go in the hospital September fifteenth for a scheduled test to see if my brother's lung is compatible, and I would like to have as much done before then."

"So soon," Bridget said. "I thought that would be much further on down the road."

"No, I had a bout during summer that made me realize the quicker I can have this done the better off I will be."

"What happened?" asked Bridget.

Sister Calista went on to tell her about the library incident and how her brother came and stayed with her. "He really is a great guy. It must be a good feeling to have a brother, someone close to you that you can count on."

"It sure is." Sister said upon rising from the bed and heading for the door. She didn't want to get into any more family conversation. "I'll let you get settled in. I'm sure you understand the urgency, given what I have just told you."

"Oh yes, and if there is anything I can do please let me know."

The door closed with Sister standing on the opposite side hoping there wouldn't be any need.

"Looks great," said the doctor, pleased with the words he spoke to both Tim and Sister Calista. "There is a match, and whenever you two can set up a date, we can look at performing the transplant."

The news could not have made the two of them more happy. They were side by side in the recovery room after the biopsy and talked excitedly about how fortunate they were. Prior to going to the hospital, they spoke very little, afraid of showing their fear. The few days of waiting seemed endless. The silences between them when they were together depressed them both.

Conversation seemed stinted with caution on both sides not to talk about the what ifs. Now that was behind them and they both couldn't stop talking, just like they always did about anything and everything.

"My schedule can work around yours," said Tim. "I can be more flexible on a date."

"That's great. I think the sooner the better. How about the first week in October? This way I can have time to recover before the debate in November."

"No problem. I'll let my superiors know, and when the doctor gives you the exact date you can let me know. As long as I know it will be the first week in October, I can leave my schedule free for that week."

The nurse came in and told them both they were free to leave. Tim went into another room to offer privacy to Sister while she dressed.

The drive back to school was exhilarating for Sister Calista. She felt like she had been given a new lease on life. Thoughts of Bridget came to mind as she hummed one of her favorite tunes. "Thank you God, thank you God." She mumbled in between notes.

The scheduled date for the operation was October second. Not too much time to complete all the debate work, but with the help of her students, Sister allocated arguments necessary for them to practice among themselves. She was pleased with the work they had done over the summer months, and, upon reading all the materials the students presented her with, she was able to work up marvelous arguments. Days were filled with getting other teachers to handle her course assignments while in the hospital, and when night came she usually fell into bed exhausted.

One morning she awakened sweating profusely. The dream she had upset and puzzled her. She had dreamt Bridget's grandmother was standing on a cloud beckoning to her. Her right hand held up and with her index finger, she kept beckoning almost like one would do if they wanted a person to come closer to hear what they had to say. Why on earth would she ever dream of that woman? Then she remembered seeing the picture of her in Bridget's dorm room. *It's amazing how the mind works*, she thought to herself as she poured her coffee that morning and tried to dismiss the upsetting dream.

The morning of the operation Tim called and asked if he could pick her up and they could drive to the hospital together. She was glad that she didn't have to go in alone and said that it would be great.

"This is the big day," he said to her while helping her place her bag in the back of the car.

"Scared, I'm scared, Tim." Her eyes started to fill up with tears.

"Now, don't be afraid." He hugged his sister and reassuringly tried to comfort her. "This is an operation that's commonplace today. It's not like we're the first to go through this kind of surgery. It's been performed over and over, and just think how fortunate we are to be able to help each other. There are plenty of people out there not as fortunate as we are." He struggled to find the words that would help them both get through this moment.

"It's true. Everything you're saying is true, but I can't help think of what I'm asking you to do, putting your life in danger."

"Don't be ridiculous. People have lived out long and healthy lives with only one lung. I'm only glad that it was me that was the one compatible. I don't know how I would have fared if I couldn't have been able to do this for you."

"You're wonderful." She got into the car and they drove off to the hospital.

Chapter Eleven

Sister Calista was not the only one whose curiosity was aroused. Julia was present when Bridget and Patricia mentioned their thoughts about Georgia O'Keeffe's charcoal paintings. Labor Day weekend, when the girls returned from the beach and settled on the huge wraparound, open air porch to discuss their notes on the upcoming debate, their conversation disturbed Julia's tranquility.

"There may be something you can use in your summation; after all, you were assigned viability." Patricia was referring to the girls both agreeing that the abstract drawings were very similar to a sonogram of an unborn fetus. "Summations allow for latitude in the presentation of facts and opinions, no matter how far-fetched. If they can tie into the viability angle, it can give strength to your argument."

"Paintings—emotional responses one feels on viewing someone's art—is going to be a hard sell."

"Maybe not, Bridget. If we saw a resemblance of flowing life in O'Keeffe's work who's to say some others wouldn't re-think the issue, especially if they are women?"

Julia usually sat in a lounge chair, away from the girls, so as not to disturb them, but she was in hearing range to all they said. Why did Bridget join that debating team anyway? Julia put down the book she was trying to read, but the girls' talk upset her. Her mind would start to wander back to when she first realized she was pregnant and all the uncomfortable things that happened after the discovery. She wanted to forget that part of her life. All this talk about viability and fetuses resurrected painful times in her life. How could someone's art influence anyone's opinion about such a personal matter?

The question resurfaced after Bridget left for school and Julia found herself scouring the library for books on the famous painter. They were strewn about the coffee table. Clifford came into the living room, sat down on the sofa, and gently pushed some of them to one side.

"I see Bridget is not the only one interested in O'Keeffe." Julia wished she had put them away before he came home that evening. She didn't feel like discussing her reasons for getting the books. Any conversation about her abortion of years ago usually ended in her crying and Clifford apologizing for having influenced her decision.

Julia had spent the afternoon reading O'Keeffe's letters and looking through picture books of works by the famous painter. It was the abstract charcoal drawings, however, that had an eerie effect on her. They reminded her of the signs right-to-life advocates carried, banners with unborn babies at various stages. These signs upset Julia; when pro-life groups asked her to participate in demonstrations, she would decline if leaders of the group said there would be such advocacy present.

"Where on earth did you get all of them?" Clifford picked one up and started turning its pages.

"Most of them came from the library, a few I picked up at Barnes and Noble at the mall."

"She certainly liked large."

"I suppose so but…" it was on the tip of her tongue to blurt out how she felt about the abstract charcoal drawings compared to what the girls had seen, but she knew it would develop into an old argument, so she added, "I was curious about her work after the girls talked about it over the holiday."

Tim was glad to be home. Sister Calista didn't recuperate as fast as her brother. The first day after the surgery her medication to regulate any rejection of the implant didn't please her surgeon. Tim bounced back quickly, the doctors gave him a clean bill of health and ordered his release.

The car trip home tired him. When he flipped on his telephone answering machine, a familiar voice came on. "Heard you were going to be let out today," the voice of Father Paul, his buddy and fellow teacher at Fordham University, echoed in the small apartment. "You're on for a decent meal tonight. Italian, my treat, after all that hospital food. Call me." He smiled at his friend's invitation. His mail was stacked beside the phone. Father Paul had placed it there daily. Tim rifled through it, nothing earth shattering; he picked up the phone and rang up his friend.

"I'm home; thanks for the invite, I'm really tired, though. I'll catch some shut-eye and see you about seven. Where are we going? Great, sounds good, I'll see you there about seven." He went into his bedroom and didn't bother to undress. He flopped on his bed and in a matter of minutes was off to sleep.

A sudden clap of thunder woke Tim: The room was in darkness except when lightning streaked across and illuminated his back wall. He reached over to look at the clock; it was six ten; he'd better get moving. He showered, shaved, and changed his clothes. The surgery made it difficult for him to move. There was a long incision in his back that the doctors made when removing his organ, and his doctor told him there would be soreness on his left side when he raised it. This reminder was evident as he tried to put his shirt on. *I hope this doesn't last too long*; and looked out the window at the pelting rain and picked up his raincoat.

He couldn't find a parking space outside the restaurant, so he circled the block a few times. The rain had stopped and he hoped he would luck out at someone leaving, but it didn't happen. He had to park several blocks away. No sooner had he put the key in the lock than a hand struck his left ear with the command, "Don't turn around."

The action happened quickly. There were two assailants. The one who struck his ear advised him he would be dead if he didn't give up his wallet.

"No problem." Tim reached into his jacket pocket, and as he did his white collar became exposed.

"What have we here, a priest?" one of the assailants mocked. "What dumb luck...can't imagine a windfall in *his* wallet."

When Tim handed over the wallet, he turned just in time to see a tattoo on the grasping hand receiving it. "I told you not to turn around," and another blow sent him to the ground. When he came to his senses, he realized he was bleeding profusely. Staggering toward the restaurant, disheveled and bloody, people stood away from him. At the restaurant door he collapsed. People coming out shouted to the patrons inside to call for an ambulance, and at the ruckus, Father Paul came to the entrance as well, looking down at his friend lying in the doorway.

Father Paul pushed himself through the crowd to be at his friend's side. "What happened, Tim? Can you hear me? Give me something to stop this bleeding." Someone handed him several napkins. Finally, the ambulance arrived and took him and his friend to Fordham Hospital.

"There's been another mugging just off the Grand Concourse. You would think these guys would let up in the rain," the police sergeant found himself talking out loud, "and a priest no less." He picked up the phone. "Mulligan, we have another mugging; a priest on his way to dinner was mugged and beaten pretty badly. They took him to Fordham Hospital. Get over there and see if it's the same guys who worked over those others last week. It's the same neighborhood." The officer put down the phone mumbling incoherently his disgust with hearing about the recent mugging.

"Are you a relative?" Detective Mulligan asked Father Paul as he paced back and forth outside the emergency room. "Could you tell me what happened?"

"I'm not sure. I wasn't with him when he was assaulted. We had planned to have dinner at the restaurant about seven, and the next thing I know, there's all this commotion, and my friend is lying in the doorway of the place bleeding profusely. He's not in the best of health right now. He has just given a lung to his sister, a nun up in Connecticut. He just got out of the hospital today after major surgery. That's about all I can tell you."

"Doctor?" The detective caught the arm of the doctor leaving the cubicle. "How's the priest doing? Will he pull through?"

"He's lost a lot of blood, hopefully he won't go into shock." The doctor looked down at the hold the detective had on his arm, and the doctor's eye contact released the hold.

"When will I be able to question him?"

"That's pretty hard to tell," said the doctor. "He's in a weakened condition because of his recent surgery, and this trauma to his system only adds additional stress."

The detective turned to Father Paul. "Do you intend to stay until you can see him?"

"Yes, I'll have to call the college and let them know as well. What more can happen to this poor guy? First he loses out on the chance of a lifetime to go to Rome and study for a year, then his sister needs a transplant, and now this; he gets mugged going out to dinner." The young priest shook his head in disbelief.

"You're right; it seems bad things happen to a lot more good people than makes the papers. Hopefully, your friend is strong enough to pull through this ordeal." The detective no sooner finished his remark than the emergency door swung open and a host of doctors and nurses clamored around the gurney with Father Tim. The medical team brushed against Father Paul as they sped down the corridor of the hospital. "What's going on?" The detective questioned the lone attendant closing the emergency door.

"They have to perform surgery on him; he's lost too much blood. The attendant disappeared behind the door. The two men looked at each other in disbelief at the quick turn of events.

"Where's the operating room?" Father Paul wasted no time in finding out. He ran down the hall after the medical team, stopping at the front desk, with the detective trailing close behind.

"Third floor, but you might as well stay down here; you'll be advised how the patient is doing when the operation is over." The nurse's response sounded cold and uncaring to Father Paul, and the detective tried to comfort him.

"She's right, no use going up there. I'll wait with you down here. Would you like a cup of coffee? Something to eat? It's probably going to be awhile."

"No thanks, but I'm going to have to find a phone and call the college." The two men inquired as to where to find a phone and the coffee shop.

Two hours passed before word came down about the condition of the priest. The news wasn't good. The priest had expired on the operating table. One of the doctors came down to the front desk and spoke to Father Paul and Detective Mulligan.

"Now we have a mugging turned into a murder," said the detective to the visibly distraught priest. "Did he say anything to you at all, Father, in the ambulance while on the way to the hospital? Anything at all. I want to catch these guys and put them away."

"There was one thing. I don't know if it will be a help. He was pretty delirious, but he mumbled something: 'I shouldn't have turned around, but then the tattooed fingers wouldn't show.' It didn't make much sense. Maybe one of these guys had a tattoo on his hand or fingers."

"Let me make a note of it." The detective took out a small notebook and jotted it down. "Anything at all can help in tracking these vermin down. You said his sister is still in the hospital in New Rochelle? I'll have to make a trip up there and notify her. It's something I'm not looking forward to. Can I give you a lift back to the college?"

"No thanks," Father Paul said, turning toward the exit sign. "Who would have believed this night?" The distraught young man shook his head and disappeared into the night.

"I'll find those lowlifes," the detective mumbled to himself. "I'll find them if it's the last thing I do." He slipped the notebook into his pocket.

Chapter Twelve

The swarming medical teams around the ailing priest the night before and the intensive questioning of Father Paul had left little time for Detective Mulligan to reflect on the victim's name: *O'Connor*. But he thought about it during the drive up to New Rochelle as the car lapped up mile after mile. Names could sometimes pluck unsolicited memories from one's past.

"Una never mentioned a sister in the convent, though she did mention a brother studying for the priesthood." He found himself talking aloud. "Wonder what ever happened to her?" He flipped on the car radio.

"The fabulous fifties." The disc jockey named a list of songs that would air in the next hour. The detective smiled.

"How about that?" he said, still talking to himself. The songs awakened old memories of times spent with Una many years before. He hummed along with the lyrics of some of the ones he remembered, and then, like a bolt of thunder, he grasped the wheel, thinking of the last phone call he had made to her after his marriage. Whatever had possessed me to do that? What had I been thinking of? He remembered having an argument that day with Jean and feeling sorry for himself, given the circumstances of his wedding.

They had just finished supper. It had been three months since Andrew and Jean had tied the knot. "It looks like we're in for a heavy thunder shower." Jean rose from the kitchen table and went around the tiny three-room apartment shutting windows.

"Why must you do that?" Andrew said. "It's only going to make it hotter in here than it already is."

"Well, I don't want the rain coming in on floors that we just had sanded and varnished."

"That's another thing you did without asking me. Why should we have that done? Who knows how long we're going to be here."

"What do you mean, 'another thing'?" Jean glared at him visibly upset by his remark.

"Putting a deposit on this apartment. I never would have agreed to living here. It's too small. And with the baby due soon, we'll have to hunt around for a house."

Jean retreated into the bedroom and threw herself down on the bed sobbing.

"You never could make up your mind about anything," she cried, face down. "If I hadn't said we're going to have a baby, you would still be running around with...that Una O'Connor or...someone else."

"I'm sorry, Jean." Andrew, shocked by her knowledge of his affair with Una, was caught off guard. He sat down next to her, but no amount of consolation or remorse on his part seemed to have any effect. She sat up in the bed and screamed at him that she *wasn't* pregnant, that she had gotten tired of waiting around for him to set a date. She pounded on his chest.

He pushed her away, stood up, and walked out of the room. Any guilt he had felt about Una left. After all, she was the one who had tricked him into thinking he was to become a father. Why else would he have moved up the wedding date? He wondered if Una ever married and had kids. That night he slept on the couch, and thoughts of Memorial Day weekend crept into his dreams.

Arriving at the hospital, Andrew checked at the front desk and asked about Sister Calista's doctor. He knew the news of her brother's death would be a shock to the nun, and he wanted a doctor around if there was a need for one. The doctor was concerned too after he heard the news.

"I'll walk down the hall and show you her room. There's another nun in there now with her helping her packing getting ready for discharge. I'll send a nurse down in case there is need for me." The doctor poked his head in the door, announcing the arrival of the police officer, and was gone. Sister Calista's companion had her back to the door and was gathering flower arrangements and plants, but the patient faced the door.

"Sister Calista." The detective addressed the two, but it was Sister Calista whose eyes he met. They recognized each other, but in the presence of the third party they said nothing.

"I'm afraid I have bad news about your brother, Father Tim."

"Oh no, what is it? Has he been hurt? Is he in the hospital? What happened?" Her questions came rapidly even as she staggered against the bed, grasping the mattress for support. The sight of Andrew after all these years, then hearing that her brother was in trouble, had sent her reeling. The other sister called for a nurse, and immediately the doctor who had offered his assistance entered the room.

"Please, Sister, let us help you," said the doctor, helping her back into her bed. "I'm going to give you a sedative to help you deal with this."

"Wait," she pleaded, "I want to know what happened to my brother, please."

Never expecting the scenario, Andrew haltingly went on with the rest.

"Your brother was mugged in New York while on the way to meet a friend of his, Father Paul. They were going to have dinner in a restaurant on the Concourse. He was taken to Fordham Hospital, and complications set in during an operation. He died on the operating table. I'm so sorry, Sister, for your loss."

The doctor quickly administered her a shot and advised all in the room to leave. The shock of this unexpected news, along with the messenger delivering it, had caused Sister Calista to faint. The nun who had been helping her was now in tears outside the room, talking to the detective.

"She was doing so well," the nun said in between sobs. "Now, with this horrible news, who knows what will happen. They were so close."

"Is that the only family she has?" Mulligan asked.

"As far as I know. Their parents are both dead, and I have never heard her speak about any others," the nun volunteered.

"I'll stay here for awhile if you want to go back to the college and inform them. I'm sure Sister Calista will want to know more, and if I can be of any assistance to her, I would like to do that."

"Thank you, officer, that's kind of you." By now the nun had gained some composure. "The college will certainly want to know, and Sister Calista is hardly up to making funeral arrangements in her condition. She'll need all the help she can get." As she walked away, Mulligan found himself alone with his thoughts.

When did she go into the convent? And am I the cause of it? The fling in City Island, we were so young. Could it have sent her into a religious order? The normal police routine of advising the next of kin about the death of a loved one took on another dimension. She would have a difficult time dealing with her brother's death; seeing him after so many years had come as a shock as well. Hopefully, she would allow him to be of some help during this difficult period.

He didn't notice the doctor approaching until he spoke. "If you're going to wait around for Sister to wake, you'll have awhile. The sedative I gave her was strong. She'll be out for at least two or three hours, so if you want to come back or go get lunch somewhere, go ahead."

"Maybe I'll do just that," he said to the physician. He asked where the coffee shop was and headed in its direction. Mulligan felt very much alone in the cafeteria even though doctors and nurses talked animatedly around him. He thought about Una, who years ago had filled him with happiness but now lays upstairs in a hospital bed. Guilt about the part he had played in her life bombarded him. The thoughts he had about her while driving up to the hospital had never included the possibility of a religious life. Una, fun-loving, beautiful, smart—whoever would have thought she would enter a convent?

And gnawing at his conscience was the notion that he had caused it all. He sat there for a long time.

When Mulligan returned upstairs to Sister Calista's room, there were several women milling around in the hall. The doctor came out, announcing that it would be in the best interest of his patient if visitors would go in one at a time and stay briefly. He explained this news had had a very bad effect on her.

The nun who had been in the room the day before approached the detective and he spoke.

"Are all these women from the college?"

"Yes, some are teachers and some are students. There was a news bulletin on TV this afternoon that mentioned the horrible incident about Father Tim's death. It didn't take long before the entire campus heard, and many of the students are upset, especially the ones who had her in their classes. We—some of the faculty who are here—wish to offer our help to Sister in handling the funeral arrangements. Father Tim's superiors have spoken to us and are waiting for instructions."

Bridget and Patricia were among the many students anxious to see how Sister was doing.

"I know you students want to offer your condolences to Sister," said one of the older women, "but for now, she does need her rest to regain her strength, and so I would ask all of you to leave. The doctor believes it would be in her best interest. Thank you, girls." The detective watched the mournful departure of the crowd of women.

"Did you see the afternoon news bulletin?" the librarian asked Julia as she piled her return books on the desk. Julia had spent a restless night and was glad there were no other patrons. At breakfast Clifford mentioned her tossing and turning and asked how she felt. She wasn't about to tell him that the nightmares she experienced prior to her breakdown had begun again.

"No, why? Did I miss something important?"

"It's just awful—a priest, mugged in New York while on his way to dinner, died as a result of his injuries. And if that's not bad enough, he had just donated a lung to his sister, who's a nun teaching at the College of New Rochelle." The five-inch TV perched on the librarian's desk station had the volume turned down, but a news broadcast was about to start.

"Would you mind turning the volume up? My daughter goes to that college."

"Oh, my God." Julia let out a gasp and covered her mouth. The split TV screen showed pictures of Sister Calista and Father Tim.

"You know these people?" the librarian asked.

"Did they mention the priest's name?"

"O'Sullivan. No that's not it…O'Connor—yes his name was O'Connor. Tim O'Connor."

"It can't be." Julia's eyes widened. Her reaction made the librarian wish she hadn't said a word. "It can't be. Bridget loves that nun, this will make her love her even more." Julia's eyes widened as she rattled on incoherently. "This is punishment, punishment for me. Now I will lose two babies."

"Whatever do you mean, Mrs. Clark? What babies?" By now the librarian was completely puzzled.

"You don't understand," Julia said, raising her voice; then she turned and ran from the library. Mumbling to herself, she stabbed the air with her arms and fingers while running towards her car. In a frenzy, she flung open the car door and struggled to fit the key in the ignition of her car. "I have to go to this woman and ask her not to take my daughter from me." Julia headed for the Garden State Parkway. "I must take Bridget out of school; I must take Bridget out of school," she kept repeating to herself.

Unlike the last time, when her husband Clifford had helped her in the safety of her home, guiding her toward medical help, she was alone as her thoughts spiraled out of control. She approached a toll booth, but instead of depositing money she raced her car around all the toll booths and sped on her way. The toll booth attendant stared in dismay as her car raced up the parkway. It wasn't long before a patrol car was in pursuit. With sirens screeching and cars moving over to the slow lane, Julia ignored the police and drove even faster, changing lanes as she evaded them.

"The APs are in," Les, the managing editor, hollered over to the copy editors. He scanned the text and said aloud, "What next? Would you believe a priest, just after giving his sister a new start on life by donating his lung, was mugged and killed by some dirt-bags on his way to dinner?"

"Let me see that" said Clifford, passing the desk. The editor handed the copy to his boss. Along with the story, there were pictures of the priest and his sister. "Oh no," he shouted.

"What's the matter?" Les asked. "Know the people?"

"The nun…she's one of Bridget's teachers," he said, looking closer before racing toward the door. "I've got to get home. Was this on the afternoon news? Does anyone know if this info was on TV yet?" Clifford was waving the bulletin in the air to the puzzlement of his managing editor, Les.

"I guess so, boss," Les said. "Once it's on the wires, TV stations pick it up."

"Take over," he shouted.

Detective Mulligan stood next to the nun, who had just asked the crowd of visitors to leave.

"Will you have to ask her any more information?"

"Just some minor details for the record. I won't stay too long. I know it's been a terrible ordeal for her." He wanted to add the words "and me as well" but didn't. He knew he had to speak to her alone. The blinds were drawn in the room, allowing for very little light. He approached Una's bed, and she turned her head toward the approaching visitor.

"Andrew, Andrew Mulligan...is that you?" Groggy from the sedative, she whispered, "Is that you?"

"Yes, its' me, Una."

She raised her head and tried to sit up. The sound of her birth name did not evoke the same warm, comforting feeling in her as the day when her brother, Tim uttered it to console her after he found out about her sickness. Anger coursed through her being.

"Is it true? About Tim? Is he really dead, or did I dream all that?"

"No, it's all true. There was a mugging and your brother died as a result of it. It never dawned on me he was your brother. I remember that years ago you mentioned a brother studying for the priesthood. But when Father Paul told me Tim had a sister in the convent, I never made the connection. I am so sorry for your loss." Sister Calista lay back on the pillow sobbing quietly. "I'd like to—"

"Please, leave; I'd like to be alone," she said, interrupting any explanation Andrew was about to make. Her anger had not subsided and she was too weak both physically and mentally to deal with this bad news. "My brother's funeral is the day after tomorrow, and I want to attend, so I must rest."

"I understand," he said and left the room.

Chapter Thirteen

"Anyone home?" Clifford hollered, closing the front door behind him. He threw his keys on the table in the entrance hall and raced through the downstairs. The silence was a dead give-away that Julia was nowhere in the house. He veered into the living room. "She must be at the library." His eyes noticed the huge pile of books gone from the coffee table and dashed toward the front door, grabbing for his keys.

"Yes Mr. Clark, Mrs. Clark was in this morning." The librarian hesitated, then added, "Ah, well, I don't know how to say this but—"

"But what?" interrupted Clifford.

"Well, I mentioned to her the news bulletin about the priest being mugged in New York, and it seemed to upset her terribly. It seems she made some connection with your daughter and the news, and, well, quite honestly, she ran out of here in a terrible state."

"Did she mention where she was headed?"

"Well, it didn't make much sense to me, but she kept repeating over and over something about your daughter and babies. To be very honest, it just didn't make any sense to me at all—then she ran out the door."

"Thank you." Clifford knew she would head straight for Bridget, so he rushed home to make a call to the college and warn his daughter of what to expect.

"Hi, Dad, how are you? To what do I owe this unexpected midday call?" She sounded amused. Then she heard his tone of urgency as he related that her mother might be headed up to the school.

"What do you mean *might* be headed?" she asked, puzzled by his news.

"It's a long story, and as I said I can't explain over the phone. Just be aware that if she arrives there, she'll be in a very emotional state. I know this is very upsetting to you, honey, what with one of your favorite teachers going through a terrible ordeal of losing her brother and now this news about your Mother. But I'm on my way up, and I'll explain everything when I get there."

"What in the world is going on with my family?" she said aloud. Puzzled by her father's call and his bizarre explanation of what had caused her mother's emotional state, Bridget sat on her dorm bed for a long while and just stared into space.

"Cliff, I was trying to reach you." Les didn't allow his boss to finish his phone greeting. "You've got to get to Community Memorial Hospital right away. Julia was involved in an auto accident on the Garden State Parkway."

Clifford had just finished talking to Bridget when he called his office to let them know he wasn't coming back. From the description the librarian had given him about Julia's condition, he only hoped the accident was minor and no one was seriously hurt. He never expected to be interviewed by the police upon arrival at the hospital.

"Your wife, Mr. Clark, was involved in a high-speed chase on the Garden State Parkway," the officer posted outside Julia's door in the hospital said. "She went through a toll gate; rather, she circumvented a toll booth station, according to the police report, and sped on her way."

"Officer, my wife's bizarre behavior was due to shock." Clifford tried to push past the police officer to gain entrance into his wife's room. "She had been recovering from a nervous breakdown when news of someone's death triggered a relapse. Please, I'd like to see my wife."

"I'll need to talk to her when she regains consciousness," the officer insisted as Clifford pushed the door open and entered Julia's room.

She lay very still in the bed. Tubes plugged almost all visible parts of her body. Her eyes were closed and blackened. Shocked by the scene, he broke down and sobbed.

"Julia...Julia," he whispered through his tears. He tried to grasp her hand but there were too many intravenous needles, so he gently stroked her face. "What have I done to you? You never wanted to have that abortion. It was me. Me and my dreams. It never occurred to me what was right and good. You have had to suffer for what I wanted. And now Bridget will find out just how selfish I was. If you can hear me, Julia, please forgive me." The doctor entered the room and asked him to come outside.

"Your wife's condition is very serious. She has internal injuries in addition to head injuries. The next twenty-four hours will be crucial. We will know more then, and hopefully she will regain consciousness. I'm sorry, but that's all we can do for her now."

The police officer overheard the conversation and realized there would be no questioning Mrs. Clark. The officer, upon seeing the condition of Clifford, told him that he would return for information for his report and he too left. Clifford knew he had to call Bridget and tell her what had happened. He then returned to his wife's bedside and wept uncontrollably.

Father Tim's funeral was held in St. Thomas's Church not too far from Fordham University. Sister Calista recovered enough to be able to attend. At the last night of the wake, she was surprised that Bridget had not made an appearance. Patricia, Bridget's friend, knew about Bridget's mother being involved in an accident. Bridget had told her of her father's strange phone call and that he then called her back to let her know about the accident. Patricia didn't want to upset Sister further, so she didn't volunteer any information.

The church was packed with friends and students. Tim was a favorite among the faculty as well as the student body. After the funeral, the college administration invited all those at the gravesite to Leeds Hall for refreshments. Detective Mulligan was among the mourners at the gravesite. Sister Calista noticed him as she entered the limousine that would take her back to the university.

"I would like to offer my condolences for your loss," he said as she approached Sister. She looked at him; the gray around his temples did not hinder his good looks. His blue eyes focused on her, pleading for forgiveness for his behavior of long ago, the same eyes that years ago had led her to believe she was the one and only true love of his life.

"I forgave you a long time ago, Andrew. But it always puzzled me why you never had the courage to tell me about marrying Jean."

"After that night in City Island, Jean called and told me she was pregnant. It wasn't true, but at the time I believed her, and well, that's why the wedding took place so quickly. It wasn't until a few months later that I found out that she lied about the pregnancy and that was the day I made that phone call to you. I know now how unfair and selfish it was of me, but at the time I was so angry."

A mourner interrupted, and Andrew stepped aside while he and Sister spoke. When the mourner had left, Andrew turned back to her and tried to explain in detail his selfish reasons for the long-ago phone call, but Sister cut him off. "No need, Andrew; that was a long time ago and the past is the past." She had no intentions of telling him about Bridget. Why involve him now, after all this time, when she is a grown woman, secure in a loving family? No, he doesn't deserve to know. Sister wanted to conclude her business with him. "Right now, I would like only for you to find out who is responsible for my brother's death."

After receiving the phone call from her father telling about her mother's accident, Bridget immediately called Patricia and headed for the hospital. Motorists speeding along the parkway kept Bridget focused on driving and not wondering why Father Tim's death propelled her mother into a frenzy that landed her in the hospital. Upon arrival, she found her father asleep at his wife's side.

"Dad," she whispered and gently stroked her father's hand.

"Bridget," he stood and backed up toward the doorway. "I'm so glad you're here. Your mother is in serious condition and the next twenty-four hours will be crucial."

"I don't understand. Why was she coming up to school? What was it that upset her so when she heard about Father Tim's terrible murder?"

Her father looked over at his wife in the bed and saw no change. He motioned for Bridget to come out into the hall. "Come, let's get a cup of coffee; I have something to tell you that perhaps your mother and I should have told you long ago and maybe, just maybe, some of this could have been avoided." Father and daughter proceeded to the coffee shop where Clifford told his daughter all about how she came to be adopted. "And you see, when you came home from school and brought up the fact you were going to be in a debate all about the abortion issue, well, old skeletons started to reappear in our lives."

"You mean that there is a possibility that Sister Calista may…may be my birth mother?"

"I'm sure that's what your mother believes. Of course, there is the possibility of coincidence, but that's something we would have to ask."

Julia's condition, along with the news about her birth mother, shocked Bridget she turned ash white and fainted.

The intern, who came to Bridget's aid, handed her a drink of water. "There, you took a nasty spill," he said as he looked up at her forehead. "Why don't you come back to the emergency room just down the hall and I'll take a look at it."

Bridget felt embarrassed by the stares of the patrons and declined the offer. Her father guided her outside and away from the staring glares. "Do you want a doctor to take a look at that cut on your forehead?"

"No, it's nothing; I'll be all right. It's…its' just I'm so confused and scared."

"There's no need for you to feel that way, honey." He hugged his daughter. "I know it's a lot to deal with all at once, but we're family and we'll get through this; you'll see." He hugged his daughter again, and they walked back to Julia's room.

Chapter Fourteen

The nurse set up two cots in Julia's room. When Bridget and her father entered, she mentioned that both of them could spend the night.

"Why don't you go home," Clifford whispered to his daughter. "I'll call you if there is any change in your mother's condition." Bridget looked down at the bed with the mention of *"mother."*

Her head started to ache when she approached Julia's bedside, and tears welled up in her eyes. "Don't cry, Bridget," Her father embraced her as she spun around and crushed herself against his chest. "We'll get through this," he added. "You go home. I'll be alright here and let you know if there is any change."

Bridget separated herself from the embrace and haltingly said she would do just that. She wanted time to sort out all that had happened to her and welcomed her father's suggestion. It was only a short drive to her home, and upon arrival she immediately took a hot shower, downed two aspirins, and made a cup of tea. The unexpected news about her birth gave rise to memories of incidents up at the college between Sister Calista and herself. She felt secretly observed without her knowledge; betrayed because of her genuine likeness towards Sister. She needed to confide in someone outside the loop.

The phone rang and the welcome voice of her friend Patricia started to inquire about Julia's condition. Patricia could tell from Bridget's voice how upset she was and tried to calm her in between sobs.

"Oh, Pat it's so good to hear from you; I'm a basket case."

"It's been a terrible ordeal for your family. Is there anything I can do?"

It was so natural for her best friend to offer help in time of her need. In the short time the girls had been in school a warm and natural friendship developed. The weekends Patricia spent at the shore, and in Washington, cemented a common bond between them both. They spent a great deal of time together gathering information on the upcoming debate. *The debate; whoever thought my involvement would stir up secrets of so long ago?*

"My mother is still unconscious, and oh, that's not the worst of it," she cried into the phone.

"What do you mean, Bridget? Would you like me to come down? I don't have any classes until Monday."

"Could you, Pat? I can't think straight."

"Not to worry, I'll head out as soon as I hang up, and I'll see you in a while. Shall I go to the hospital or your house?"

"My house; my father is at the hospital, and he will call if there is any change in her condition." Knowing her friend would soon be at her side comforted her somewhat as she hung up the phone.

Before she headed back to the college, Sister Calista knew she had to clear up Tim's apartment. It was a job she wasn't looking forward to, but it had to be done. After the last mourner left Leed Hall, the president of the university offered his condolences and asked her if there was anything he could do for her.

"I would appreciate a ride over to my brother's apartment, if you could arrange that."

"I'll get in touch with Father Paul; I'm sure he wouldn't mind. Come in to my office and I'll see if I can get a hold of him."

"Sure, be glad to. I'll be right there." Father Paul responded to his superior's telephone request.

"There," the president sighed as he offered Sister a chair in his office, "he won't be long; he has an apartment right here on campus."

"Thank you, as long as I'm down here I might as well not put it off."

"It will be difficult for you, but you're right. The healing process begins when one comes to terms with reality."

"I hope so, Father," she replied. *How many times must Tim have been in this very same office, sat in this very same chair?* Sister smoothed the leather on the arm of the chair. The priest realized by her behavior she would rather not make small talk and took leave, begging another appointment. The silence allowed her to indulge in her brother's funeral service. *Wonder why Bridget wasn't at the wake or funeral? Patricia never mentioned anything, hope she is all right.* Her thoughts were interrupted by Father Paul's greeting.

"Hello, I'll be glad to drive you over to the apartment, and when you're done, I'll take you home to the college."

"That won't be necessary; I can rent a car."

"I wouldn't hear of it. It's the least I can do for my friend. I'll give you my phone number and when you're ready, just call."

"Thank you, all right, if you insist." They both left the office.

Sister had trouble turning the key in the lock, since the key had never been used before. Tim had given the spare key to her in case of emergency. She never thought it would be used to cart his personal belongings away. Finally, Sister gained admittance and felt her brother's presence. Familiar photos of family and friends scattered throughout the rooms resurrected their past life. Tears flowed gently down her cheeks as she fingered his jacket and the shirts in his closet.

His dresser had mail on it that hadn't been opened. The usual bills, Visa, electric, telephone; she would have to notify those companies of his death. One letter addressed to him from Trinity College, Dublin Ireland, caught her eye. The return address, Maura McHugh, Professor of Anthropology, piqued her curiosity. Sister opened the letter.

The doorbell rang and Bridget scooted down the stairs to answer. She had just pulled on a pair of jeans and sweatshirt. *It must be Patricia*, she thought as she ran to the front door. Upon opening it, she fell into her friends' arms.

"Oh Pat, I'm so confused."

"Confused?" Puzzled, Patricia pushed her back into the hallway and closed the door behind her.

"I just found out some bizarre news about me, my mother, my father, and Sister Calista."

The laundry list of names startled her friend. "What are you talking about? Calm down." She guided her distraught friend into the living room. "Start at the beginning."

Bridget revealed all that her father had told her in the hospital. As she re-told the story, Patricia's eyes grew wider, and she could only console her friend by holding her.

"That's a lot to deal with, what with your mother…"

"It's okay; my mother is in the hospital," Bridget sensed the hesitation in Patricia's voice, "and Sister Calista will always be my teacher," She emphasized. "She looks awful. Black and blue with tubes coming out of her nose and mouth. And from what my father tells me, all this trouble started when we first started to work on the abortion debate. I never knew about my mother having a nervous breakdown while I was in Washington. It seems my parents didn't think I should know about it. My mother had been under the care of a therapist, and my father said it helped a great deal. All this abortion discussion my mother heard caused her to remember the one she had many years ago. Now I know why she is so adamant about her views on the subject. My father said she blamed the abortion for not being able to conceive."

"How does Sister Calista fit into all this, being your real mother, I mean?"

Bridget related the story surrounding her birth while Patricia listened attentively without any further interruptions.

"Evidently, after coming back from Australia, Sister Calista, whose real name is Una O'Connor, decided to leave Wall Street and go into teaching. It must have been a terrible shock to her when I showed up at school."

"Now it all makes sense." Patricia raised her eyebrows. "The interest in you, involving you in the debating club. I guess it was just as difficult for her not to be able to say anything to you. Your parents never caught on about who she was?"

"How would they? It was only when the news bulletin about Father Tim's death came over the TV that my father said this whole mess started. All I know is my mother may die and all because of me."

"Stop saying that. It's not true. If anything it's what we have been discovering all along about the long-term effects of abortion. Your mother has been haunted by a decision made years ago. And from what you've told me, she really didn't want to go through with it. So stop blaming yourself. It's just a terrible discovery to be made under such…such horrible coincidence… Sister's brother's death, her recent operation."

"Did she ask why I wasn't there? The funeral, I mean. Did you tell her about my mother's accident?"

"No, I didn't. I thought she had enough to handle with her operation and all. It would have only added more grief. And knowing what I know now I'm so glad I didn't say anything. She didn't look too good, very pale and weak looking. Have you decided to call her or…."

"Not right now, not until I know more about my mother's condition."

"I understand. Have you eaten anything? I'm starved. I could use a quick sandwich."

"I'm sorry, Pat, please come into the kitchen. I'm sure there is something in there for a sandwich. The girls went into the kitchen. Bridget sat at the table while Patricia made sandwiches and tea for both of them.

Dear Tim,
I'm so glad your lung tissue is compatible with our sister, Una.
Sister Calista looked at the envelope again and then continued to read the letter that was signed *Your sister from across the sea, Maura*. Puzzled, Sister looked to see if there were any more letters. She opened the top drawer of his dresser, and bundled together were a stack all from a Maura McHugh. One by one the letters revealed her mother's secret of long ago: Mickey Bradey, a name burned into Sister's memory from a long-ago ugly kitchen scene in the Bronx.

She placed the letters, along with photos and his personal effects, in a suitcase she found in Tim's closet. Exhausted by the discovery and the physical exertion in collecting her brother's belongings, she phoned Father Paul and waited for his arrival.

"Are you all right?" Father Paul must have recognized the anxiety in Sister's face.

"I'm glad you volunteered to drive me home. I suppose this has taken its toll on me." Father Paul picked up the suitcase she had packed and they left the apartment. "I'll give you Tim's key. There will be no need for me to keep it anymore. If you don't mind, you can call the St. Vincent De Paul Society and donate his clothes, furniture, and the rest of his belongings. If there is anything you might want, feel free to take it."

"I'll call them tomorrow and do that, but for now why don't you try to relax." He tossed the suitcase in the trunk and headed for New Rochelle.

The priest tried to make small talk but soon realized Sister barely answered, so he gave it up. She closed her eyes and tried to make sense of all she learned that afternoon. Exhausted, she drifted off to sleep. *She will certainly miss Tim, and so will I.* He looked away and was glad she had fallen asleep and couldn't see the single tear that ran down his cheek.

Patricia and Bridget headed for the hospital right after breakfast. Clifford called that morning with good news. Julia had come around and started to recognize things.

"I'm so nervous about seeing her," Bridget said as she drove to the hospital.

"You'll be fine," her friend volunteered, patting her on the shoulder.

"I'm so glad you're here, you have no idea how spaced out I was before you arrived."

"Hey, what's a friend for? I'm sure you would have done the same for me."

The parking lot was full and she had to drive around and around before finding an empty spot. The hospital buzzed with all kinds of people coming and going. "A hospital never sleeps," Patricia quipped as they both headed for the elevator. Bridget could feel her hands become sweaty as she pushed the elevator button. "Don't worry," her friend said. "You'll know exactly what to say when the time comes."

Bridget gently pushed open the door of her mother's room. Her father, upon hearing it, greeted the girls. "She started to wake up in the middle of the night. It took a while before she understood where she was, but she seems to be her old self again. She's in a lot of pain, but they try to keep it under control. She has been asking for you."

"Does she remember where she was going when all this happened?" Bridget asked her father.

"I didn't ask and all she remembers is the crash. I didn't ask her any more because with all the tubes, its' difficult to make sense of what she says."

Bridget approached Julia's bed and gently stroked her mother's hand. Her blackened eyes were now blue and a mustardy yellow. She managed a slight smile, difficult with the tube insertion in her mouth. Bridget's eyes filled with tears at the condition of her mother's helplessness.

"Oh Mom, I'm so glad you woke up. We were so afraid there for awhile." Again her mother feigned another smile.

"Sorry to cause so much trouble," her voice slurred out the words.

"Trouble…what trouble? You're the one in such pain, but thank God you came back to us. You must rest and get strong."

Patricia stood in back of Bridget, and Julia recognized her as well. "I'm glad your friend is with you," she said in barely a whispered tone. She then dozed off into a sleep.

"Dad, is she all right?" Bridget raced to her father's side. "She's fallen asleep; is that ok?"

"Yes, she wakes up periodically, and because of the heavy sedation she lapses into sleep. The doctors say it's normal in these kinds of situations. It will be a long recovery. She suffered broken ribs, and when she is well enough they have to repair internal damage."

The group went into the hallway to finish their discussion. "Thank you, Patricia, for coming down and staying with Bridget. I'm sure she appreciates your thoughtfulness at this time."

"I didn't have any classes scheduled so it was no problem at all. I'm glad to be able to be of some help. Speaking of classes, have you forgotten next week is our final rehearsal for the debate? Will you be able to come up?"

"I don't know…."

"Of course you will," her father interrupted. "You didn't do all that research and study not to finish. Your mother is on the road to recovery, and both she and I would want you to compete."

"And then there is the other…."

"I know," her father said. "Just like I had to come forward and level with you, you must have the courage to face Sister and tell her you know about your past. It doesn't change your feelings towards her. And just as it will hurt her, it may heal her as well. Her brother's death, just as your mother's accident, caused the truth to finally surface and may well be healing for us all."

"Oh, Dad, I suppose you're right. I have to face Sister and tell her. I'm sure she will understand my feelings toward you and mom. No one could ever take your place. It's just that it is such an awkward situation. I do feel so very sorry for her because of all that's happened to her—the operation, her brother's death."

"Your father's right," chimed in Patricia. "I'm sure Sister will be just as glad. It must have been difficult seeing you every day. Now that her brother is gone, she may not feel as alone knowing you know. I'm headed back to school this afternoon. Do you think you will be coming back soon?"

"I'd like some time with my mom, and I'll plan on leaving tomorrow morning. Thanks again for coming down so quickly. You certainly were a lifesaver for me."

Patricia left and headed toward the elevator, then father and daughter went back into the room.

Chapter Fifteen

After Father Paul left, Sister collapsed onto her bed. She struggled to remove her clothing and upon doing so fell into a deep sleep. A ringing phone awakened her the next morning.

"I hate to disturb you, Sister," a voice on the other end said, "There is a Mr. Hardy at the administration desk who is here to see you."

"Yes," Sister recognized the name. She sat upright in the bed saying aloud, "The bus for Washington; I forgot all about it. Please tell him I've been delayed but will be there shortly."

"Certainly," the voice on the other end said. Sister hung up the phone. To her surprise she felt better. Yesterday's surprise had taken its toll on her, but sleep seemed to revive her. It didn't take long to shower and dress.

"I'm sorry to have kept you waiting. My brother's funeral...."

"No need to explain, Sister; I've been told about your loss. I'm so sorry." He never gave her a chance to finish the sentence.

"Thank you, now if I remember correctly the bus company quoted a price of two-hundred dollars to drive to Washington and return us the next day; is that correct?"

"Yes, there are twenty-eight passengers, according to your letter," he said, looking over his paperwork.

"Correct, nine students, the rest faculty, parents, and friends."

"There is a balance of one hundred fifty dollars I'm supposed to collect this morning in order to process the trip."

"I'll have the bursar draw you a check." Sister picked up a phone at the desk and called the bursar's office, requesting the payment and would they have someone deliver the check to the administration office. Not long after, a student appeared and the appointment came to an end.

Interacting with Mr. Hardy about college business gave Sister the boost she needed to ease back into her old life. *Final rehearsal for the debate is this week, must concentrate and stay focused on that,* she thought to herself as she walked back toward her apartment. She wanted to read all those letters she found in her brother's apartment and find out more about a sister whom she just discovered.

"Hello!"

Sister turned to find Patricia running to catch up with her. "Why hello, Patricia, you're just one of the many I would like to see." She smiled at her. "Wednesday we will have our final practice for the debate. I must get in touch with the rest of the debating team. Have you seen Bridget recently?"

"Yes, I have. She didn't attend the funeral because her mother was involved in a serious auto accident last week. I didn't mention it to you at the funeral because I felt it would only add to your grief. She is recovering, and Bridget said she would return as soon as possible."

"How terrible. Was she the only one involved?"

"As far as I know. I spent the weekend with her. She was very upset." Patricia had a difficult time trying to converse with the nun, knowing about the relationship between her and Bridget.

The two women walked toward Sister's apartment, and just before they reached it Sister stopped in front of the small chapel on campus.

"I think I'll stop in for a visit; if you chance to see any of the team, remind them of the rehearsal."

"I certainly will," the student replied and went on her way.

A sense of quiet took hold of Sister as she entered the chapel. She was not alone. A woman was kneeling at the altar rail. As the woman rose, blessed herself, and turned to head down the aisle, Sister realized it was Bridget.

"Bridget, I'm so sorry to hear about your mother's accident. I just ran into Patricia and she told me." Bridget's eyes filled with tears. Sister went to embrace her, but she pulled away. Confused by her behavior, the nun was startled.

"You'll have to forgive me, Sister, but I have been under a great deal of stress these past few days."

"I understand," the nun said, still puzzled by the rejected embrace.

"My father told me my mother was on her way up here after hearing about your brother's terrible tragedy. It seems she had suffered a nervous breakdown while I was in Washington, and since she made a quick recovery they never told me." Sister Calista sat down in the pew. She felt faint. *She knows about us.* Bridget went on talking, but the nuns' weakened condition, physically and mentally, shut out most of it.

Alarmed at the radical change in Sister, Bridget forgot about all her pent-up anger and sat down next to her. "Are you all right? I'll see if I can get a drink of water." She got up and raced down to a water cooler in the vestibule of the chapel, filled a paper cup, and gingerly held it in her hand heading back into the chapel. By this time Sister had regained her composure, but her face remained ashen.

"Here, drink this," Bridget said and handed the cup to her.

"Is there no end to all this horrible news?" Sister's voice pleaded.

"My mother is on the road to recovery; it will be a long one, but nonetheless the doctors say she will make a complete recovery."

"You said she was on her way up here; why is that?"

"This is difficult for me…."

"Does it have something to do with me?" Sister begged the question, looking into Bridget's tearful eyes, and within minutes the two women were hugging each other.

Leafing through his report in the hospital corridor, the police officer pushed the down button for the elevator. The door opened and Clifford Clark stood facing him. Clifford recognized him as the same policeman who wanted to question Julia the day of her admittance.

"Mr. Clark," the officer backed into the hallway to allow others access to the elevator. "I've taken a statement from your wife." Clifford's face flushed red with annoyance.

"Couldn't it wait until she made a full recovery?" He wanted to be there when Julia regained her memory of exactly what took place.

"You must understand, I have my work to do. Her doctor informed me she was up to making a statement. I don't believe any charges will be leveled against her. I have a doctor's report that states she suffered from a chemical imbalance just before the accident, and it will be entered into the report as well."

On hearing this news, Clifford relaxed and extended his hand to the officer in a gesture of an apology. "I'm sorry if I had been short with you, but I guess you can realize the strain I was under."

"Certainly, Mr. Clark." An elevator appeared going down and the officer took leave.

Julia sat up in the bed and looked so much better than the day before. She had been up and applied makeup and did up her hair.

"You look terrific," Clifford announced as he headed toward her and landed a peck on her cheek. All the tubes had been removed; only black and blue marks remained where they had been inserted.

Julia stared down at her hands and commented, "Just look at all these black and blue marks. I could cover most of the ones on my face and neck with makeup, but the ones on my hand…uggh." She shuddered.

"You have been one lucky lady, so don't mind a few discolorations for a few days or so. Bridget drove up to school this morning and she is fine."

"That's what I've been wanting to hear about. Ever since the accident, I remember going off on a tangent when I heard about Sister Calista's brother Tim and tying the two together. Does she know? Did you have to tell her?"

"Yes, she knows and yes she was upset, but I explained to her the situation Sister was in."

"What about my having an abortion, did you mention that as well?"

"I had to, Julia. How else could I have explained what happened to you?" Julia looked away.

"Does she hate me for it?"

"No, she doesn't hate you. She just had a lot of upsetting news thrown at her and it took awhile to work her way through it all. I'm so glad Patricia came down over the weekend. I'm sure that helped her a great deal. I just ran into the police officer in the hall. He said you gave him a statement about the accident and he mentioned a doctor's report."

"Yes, my doctor had the psychiatrist fill out the necessary papers to explain the condition I experienced."

"What did he say would happen to you?"

"A suspended sentence and my driver's license revoked until I get a clean bill of health saying I'm cured."

"Well, that's good news; you'll just have to start those therapy sessions again and now I think you will make fantastic progress."

"What makes you say that?"

"There's no secrets from anyone anymore. You're not under any of that blanket of anxiety. Bridget knows the origin of her birth and it doesn't matter one bit. You're her mother. She told me so. Sister Calista is a teacher whom she is genuinely fond of but will never replace you."

"Are you sure?"

"Sure I'm sure, but she will tell you that herself. She wanted to stay but I insisted she go back to school. We talked a great deal about how she had to go on with her studies and the debate that is coming up shortly. She didn't want to go to Washington because of you, but when I saw you coming around I thought it best she go."

"You were right," Julia's face contorted.

"What's the matter?"

"Every time I move it hurts; the doctor says my ribs will take a while to heal and when the pain killers wear off every little move hurts."

"Shall I ring for the nurse?"

"No, she is due in soon. I don't want to be dependent on any drugs unless it's absolutely necessary. The sooner I can function without any can't be too soon for me. I feel so stupid creating all this unnecessary trouble for everyone. If only I hadn't heard about Sister's brother."

"It's just as well. I don't mean about your accident, but it was bound to come out sooner or later about Bridget's birth. We would have recognized

Sister when we attended the debate in Washington. The fact she kept it under wraps all this time tells me she had no intention of letting on to Bridget who she was. Any discovery made during the trip could have been almost like a sidebar one sees in a court room. While the students are involved in the debate, Sister would take us aside and tell us she had no intention of saying anything. I've had a lot of time to think about it here in the hospital waiting for you to regain consciousness."

"I hope you're right; I want to call Bridget, but I think I'll wait until I hear from her.

Bridget and Sister left the chapel and headed toward the cafeteria. Amidst all the crying they both realized how hungry they were, not having had any breakfast. The air felt refreshing as they slipped their arms together and strolled toward the building. The two women filled their trays with cereal, juice, coffee, and toast and headed for a table.

"Is your mother going to make a full recovery?" Sister had no intention of claiming that title.

"Hopefully, I spoke to her briefly when she awoke. We didn't say much; there were so many tubes…she couldn't say too much."

"How did she hear about Tim's…."

"She went to the library to return some books and the librarian mentioned it to her. When she mentioned that you were teaching up at the College of New Rochelle, it must have caused this…this chemical imbalance that causes irrational behavior. My father told me she had an abortion just before they were married. She didn't want to, but my father said he encourage it because my grandparents had planned this big wedding and to move the date up…well, my father said it was more or less his insistence and, well, I guess it's haunted her ever since. The fact that you had me and did it more or less on your own probably didn't help either."

"When I first visited your mom, I must say I was surprised how young she was to want to adopt a baby."

"All this talk about the debate I'm sure didn't help her frame of mind either. I remember some nasty scenes during the summer while Patricia visited."

"Patricia, I suppose she knows…you mentioned she visited during the weekend. I'm glad she was able to be with you when you were so upset. I know how comforting it had been for me when Tim…" Sister caught herself and tried to think ahead of letters that awaited for her at home."

"I'm sure Patricia will be discreet about this. There isn't any need for anyone else to share our news."

"No, I don't think the publicity would help the college at all, and it might even jeopardize my position here. One never knows about these things."

"I'll be seeing her later on today and ask her not to discuss it with anyone. I'm sure there will be no problem there. Have you been back to see your doctor?"

"I have an appointment at the end of this week. Given all the ups and downs I've had since the operation, hopefully, his news will be all good. It's been wonderful to talk to you in this way. You will never know the happiness I've had these past few months just watching you interact with other students, learning the art of debating." Sister Calsita's words dismissed any traces of anger Bridget felt.

Chapter Sixteen

Children scampered up and down the street in costumes, dragging various sizes of bags, announcing the ritual of Halloween. Father Paul arrived at Tim's apartment just before dusk. He wanted to spend time in a place that once was filled with many happy memories for him. He called the St. Vincent de Paul Society, and they would pick up the remainder of Tim's belongings early the next day. Since he had an early mass to say, he thought it best to make his visit without any interruptions by moving men.

"I don't think this was such a good idea," said the shorter of the two men looking over his shoulder.

"Why not? He's dead; what good is his TV and VCR?" smirked the other sarcastically. "We ring the bell and if there is no answer, we jimmy the door."

"We made a mistake, that's all. Don't hassle me anymore."

Upon seeing the two men at the door, the street-raised children running up and down the apartment stairs skipped that particular landing. The shorter man rang the bell. No answer. The taller of the two pushed him aside and started to work on gaining entrance. It didn't take long before they were looking through the closets and drawers of the man whose death they had caused.

As Father Paul went to insert the key in the lock, he noticed the splintered wood. Immediately he knew the door had been forced open. Not wanting to encounter anyone, he turned and headed down the stairs looking for the superintendent of the building. Upon finding his apartment, he rang the bell and started knocking on the door.

"Yeah, what do you want?" an annoyed woman answered.

"My name is Father Paul and I have come to clear out some of Father Tim's things. I believe someone broke into his apartment. Please call the police and ask for Detective Mulligan."

"Come in, Father." The woman turned more cordial upon hearing the circumstances. "There's the phone over there; you can call yourself. I thought you were one of those kids trick or treating. I try to keep them out, but they ring the outside bell and get in anyway. I'll be glad when this day is over."

"Yes, the priest said into the phone, paying no attention to the woman's tirade. "I don't know if there is anyone in there. I wasn't going in."

"I'll be right over; you were wise not to attempt to go in," Detective Mulligan said, lighting up a cigarette. "I think we may have the scum who did the priest," he yelled to his partner, who immediately responded, and the two officers headed out of the precinct.

"I'd like to nail those two bastards," Detective Mulligan said.

"It looks like you'll get your wish; those jerks must have thought they would clean up on his belongings as well."

"Put the siren on," Mulligan said. "I don't want them to slip through this time."

Father Paul stood outside on the street waiting. The police car attracted a small crowd. The two police officers waved the people to one side, and Father Paul met them.

"I don't know if there is anyone in there. When I saw the door had been jimmied, I called you."

"Good idea," Mulligan said. "If there is anyone in there, you might have gotten hurt."

"I thought as much; after what happened to Tim it made me think twice about playing the hero."

"You stay down here." His partner and he drew their weapons, and by now the crowd had grown and, realizing Father Paul was involved, started pestering him asking questions. The priest didn't respond to any of them and escaped back into the superintendent's apartment.

The two officers chased away the children they met on the stairs. When they reached the apartment, they both pushed the door, pointing their guns at the two unsuspecting robbers who were piling up the loot on a coffee table.

"That's all, you two; hands up," Mulligan shouted while his partner reached for his handcuffs.

"This guy has a tattoo on his hand," the officer said as he handcuffed the taller of the two.

"I told you it wasn't a good idea," the shorter assailant screamed as the officers hauled the two men out of the building. Father Paul came out of the apartment just in time to see the arrest.

"One of these birds has a tattoo," said Mulligan. "You may have to testify in court as to the conversation you had with your friend while he was alive and on the way to the hospital that night."

"Just let me know; I'd be glad to see those two put away for a long time."

"There's a pretty good chance they will be."

The priest stood on the pavement while the police car sped away. The crowd dispersed, and the children continued running in and out of apartments. *Life goes on*, the priest thought to himself, he glanced to the heavens and murmured, "Rest in peace, Tim."

The hospital volunteer peeked into Julia's room. "Is there a Mrs. Clark in here?"

"Yes," Julia responded. "That's me."

"I have quite a few cards here for you," smiled the aide.

"Wonderful, it will give me something to do with myself besides watching these insane TV shows." The volunteer left a pile of cards and letters on her bed and left the room. Julia smiled as she looked at the cards and recognized familiar names of friends. One letter caught her eye immediately. It was the name O'Connor and the return address was New Rochelle, New York. She pushed aside the other cards and picked the letter up. Her heart started to race as she tore open the envelope.

> *Dear Julia,*
>
> *By now Bridget must have told you about our long talk. It had been very emotional for both of us, but somehow or other we have resigned ourselves to our current status. She is your daughter and you will always be her mother. I'm only too happy to sit in the shadows and watch her blossom into the wonderful woman she has become. You and your husband have done an exceptional job in raising her, and for that I thank you.*
>
> *I wish you a speedy recovery and will continue to pray for all your intentions.*
> *Sincerely,*
> *Sister Calista*

Julia held the letter in her hand and reached for a Kleenex. *All that needless worrying I did*, she thought to herself. *How foolish of me*. She placed the letter back in its envelope and started to open the rest of her mail. When she came to the last of the cards, she reached for the telephone.

"Hi Mom, how are you feeling?" Bridget said.

"You sound out of breath. Were you out jogging, dear?"

"No, the phone rang as I put the key in the door and…"

"Oh, I just wanted to tell you I had a letter from Sister Calista, and she told me you two had a reconciliation."

"Yes, with all that happened to her, any feelings of anger I had stored up just fizzled. She has had enough to deal with without resentment from me. And that goes for you too, Mother. I want you to concentrate on getting better."

"I'll try, dear; by the way, how is the debate practice going? Your father tells me you are having final rehearsals."

"That's right; in fact that's where I was coming from, practice. Sister Calista is a whiz at arguments. We have a wonderful team and a pretty good chance of winning."

"I'll be rooting for you," her mother said. "Hopefully at home by that time; the doctor said I can go home the end of this week. Your father said he is going to Washington with some of the other parents."

"I know; I have been talking to him at the office. He told me you're beginning to look like your old self again. I found out the debate will be on Public Television, so you will be able to see it as well."

"I'm sure you're excited and looking forward to it."

"To be honest, I'll be glad when it's all behind me. With Thanksgiving just a couple of weeks away, I'm looking forward to the break from school and to be home with you and Dad." Julia couldn't have been happier hearing Bridget confess her innermost thoughts.

Chapter Seventeen

Bridget, although she wanted to inquire about her real father, felt uncomfortable bringing the subject up. When she and Sister Calista met in the dining hall and shared a meal, the conversation centered around the nun's life before she entered the convent.

"So, the canyons of Wall Street couldn't contain you?" Bridget said one afternoon, sliding her tray along the lunchroom table.

"No, at first I found it very exciting, but when I finished night school at Fordham and had my degree, I thought I would like to try my hand at teaching."

"Did you go into the convent right away?"

"No, I taught in the public school sector for awhile and really enjoyed working with children. After a year or two I felt a strong pull to the religious life. My brother, Tim, thought it was because I wasn't married that I decided on this path, but after many long talks with him he realized I had made up my mind."

The mention of her brother's name and the recollection of those talks she had with him caused the nun's eyes to fill with tears. Bridget knew at that point to go no further and changed the subject.

"It looks like the debating team is all set for Georgetown next week."

"Yes." Sister rallied to the switch in the conversation. "I'm so pleased with all the work the team has done. We are prepared to offer great arguments, and hopefully we'll walk away with first prize."

"That would be wonderful," Bridget agreed and picked up the tray. "Got to get going. I have a class in about five minutes."

Sister glanced at her watch, picked up her tray, and headed toward the door. The two women left the cafeteria and went their separate ways.

Leaves falling from the surrounding trees quickly filled the walkways connecting the dorms. A chilling wind swept over the campus that morning as Sister headed for her apartment after going to morning mass.

"Who could be calling me this early?" she asked as she struggled to unlock her door and race to the phone before it stopped ringing.

"We found the two who caused your brother Tim's death. They were robbing his apartment." Detective Mulligan proceeded to go into detail as to how it came about. "There was an item we recovered from one of them. It looks as if it could have been your brother's watch. There was an inscription on the back. *To Tim Love Mom.*"

"That was the watch my Mom gave him on his ordination."

"We will need it for the trial and then after that it will be released to you."

"Thanks, I would like Father Paul to have it. I'm sure Tim would have liked that, too."

"How is your recovery going? You sound pretty good. Is everything ok?"

Yes, Sister thought to herself, *and will be okay as long as you never find out about Bridget.*

"I have been pretty busy, and yes I'm feeling much, much better since I saw you last. Thank you for your help in apprehending those horrible men."

As he spoke, about Tim's assailants in custody, a peaceful calm came about her and the sound of Andrew's voice no longer disturbed her.

She wanted to spend some time re-reading the letters Maura had sent to Tim. It had been a week since the funeral, and she knew it was time to inform her about Tim. As she read the letters again, it made her curious to know more about her new-found relative. In one of the letters she had written,

Please let me know when the biopsy is done.

"Would she have volunteered her lung in the event Tim's wasn't a match? I wonder...."

Tim must have talked about growing up in the Bronx and how the lots next door to them served as the year-round playground. Maura wrote that she wished she had shared this childhood, running and climbing the makeshift ruins and sledding in the winter with them instead of pining away wondering who her parents were. His letters left out the arguments about drinking, and his words painted a somewhat idyllic childhood. Tim had a way with words.

"But Ma, you know how Dad is when he's had too much to drink. He says things he doesn't mean." Tim came home for a visit soon after his ordination and found his mother very upset about her husband's increased drinking bouts.

"I'm used to his taking too much, but the part that I can't stand is his bringing up old quarrels of long ago; I'd forgotten about them. But when he is on the ran dan, it seems that's all he can talk about it, and he can get pretty nasty, like the Mickey Bradey incident of years ago. When I tell him the next day how nasty he was, he stares out into space and says not a word."

"He's still on that. That was so long ago, Ma. Why do you think it...."

"I suppose it showed that night on my face." She started to cry.
"What showed on your face?"
"Guilt."
"What guilt? What are you talking about?" And she blurted out her secret of long ago and while at it told of Una's affair with Andrew. The priest listened while in between sobs his mother told of the long-ago secrets she had bottled up for years.

"Promise me you will not let on to Una what I told you. She swore me to secrecy. It's been…."

"Now there, shush," he whispered. "You'll feel a lot better without that load you have been carrying around with you. And as for Dad, he knows you so well he can sense that you've kept something from him. I'll speak to him and see if it can do any good."

Sister put down one of Maura's letters and gathered the rest of them into a pile. She inserted a piece of paper in her typewriter and started to type:

Dear Maura,

This is probably the most difficult letter I have ever written. Our brother, Tim, is no longer with us. He had so bravely given me his lung so as I would enjoy a better quality of life, only to lose his life in fighting off assailants who tried to rob him. He died as a result of these injuries only a few days after the lung transplant.

He recuperated faster than I did, and he was on his way to a dinner engagement with Father Paul, a close friend of his, when two men accosted him and beat him brutally. He was able to crawl to the restaurant, where an ambulance was called and he was transported to the hospital.

Possibly had he not been in such a weakened condition he would have survived, but that was not the case. The shock of Tim's death, my recovery, and the discovery of a sister has been difficult.

Evidently Tim knew more about the event surrounding your birth. My mother (our mother) must have confided in him. I would love to get to know you better. At present I'm very involved in getting students ready for a national debate next week. When that is over and I return after the Thanksgiving holiday, I would like to discuss possibly a trip to Ireland so we could meet. If this is acceptable to you, please let me know and I will make travel plans. Thank you again for all your kindness and support.

A new-found relative,
Sister Calista

Chapter Eighteen

Maura let Sister Calista's letter drop into her lap. She had been anxiously awaiting news from Tim about the results of the operation. The last letter had been almost three weeks ago and she feared the worst. Each day she parted the curtains in her front living room window, watching for the postman.

She sat in the chair staring out the window, watching the pelting rain hitting the pavement hard. Tears formed in her eyes as she picked up the letter to read it again. By the time she rose from the chair and looked at the clock on the mantle over the fireplace, she realized she had missed the bus. Usually, she took the nine o'clock at Traves Square that allowed her enough time to get to her first class at Trinity College.

"I can't teach today," she said to herself, surprised that she had spoken aloud. "Anyway, I've missed the bus." She walked into the tiny kitchen still holding the letter, reached for the phone on the wall, and started to dial.

"This is Professor Maura McHugh; I'm not going to be able to teach my class today. Would you please have someone leave messages for my students in my ten o'clock morning class as well as my two this afternoon? I've had some upsetting news from abroad about family, and I would like some time to sort it out. Thank you…no, I shall be in tomorrow. It's just that the news has come as a shock." She replaced the phone, turned toward the stove, picked up her teakettle, and proceeded to fill it.

She sat drinking her tea and thinking about the first letter from Tim. She had been shocked but not too surprised about the secrecy surrounding her birth. Growing up, Sheilah generally avoided Maura's inquisitiveness about her parents. The stock answer was she was abandoned and left on Sheilah's doorsteps. When she was a little girl, the love bestowed on her seemed enough to quell her questioning mind, but as a teenager, she had heard gossip in school surrounding her birth, raising doubts about her having been abandoned. Sheilah knew more then she was telling her.

"Are you going to Colleen's birthday party?" Sheilah asked soon after Maura received the invitation for the party Colleen's parents planned for her sixteenth birthday at the church hall.

"I wouldn't miss it for the world, Auntie." Colleen Bradey and Maura were close friends, but this relationship was one Sheilah wished never had happened. After Bridget left Glasgow, Mickey Bradey had married and had two daughters, Colleen and Kate. In a small community like Maryhill, everyone knew their neighbors and it was to be expected that the girls might become good friends. Many people seeing the two girls together almost always took them for sisters. Both had dark hair, alabaster white skin, and green eyes.

Mickey Bradey's reputation about having affairs with many of the young women in Maryhill before and after his marriage was well known. Sheilah worried that Maura might discover that he was her father, especially with the striking resemblance between Colleen and Maura. It was for this reason that Sheilah had suggested to Maura she go to Dublin to attend Trinity College. Maura was an excellent student and thrilled at the idea of studying at such a prestigious university.

This suggestion came soon after Colleen's birthday party. Mickey Bradey was drunk at the affair, much to Mrs. Bradey's embarrassment especially Colleen.

"Mom, can't you get him out of here?" Colleen pleaded in the recess outside the hall itself. Maura, close beside her friend for moral support, tried to tell her no one was paying any attention to her father. While the three women were discussing the situation, Mickey Bradey staggered past them looking for the lavatory.

"Well, what have we got here?" he spat in his drunken stupor. He fingered Maura's hair, and Mrs. Bradey shoved him away from the two young girls.

"Leave her be, you drunken lout," she shouted at her husband, fighting back tears.

"Just trying to be friendly," he slurred.

Friendly is it? You're friendly with every woman in Maryhill." Mrs. Bradey shouted at him. Maura and Colleen were able to slip back into the hall with the rest of the guests, and that night on the way home, Colleen confided in Maura about her father and the way he had been with women all his life.

"In fact," she said, "I once heard my mother accuse him of having an affair with your aunt—the one who went off to America—but because she had been married to Patrick O'Connor, the rumor soon died. Your arrival on Sheilah's doorstep seemed to be coincidental at the time."

As she rose from the kitchen table, Maura decided she would call Colleen. The two girls had kept in touch after Maura had gone off to college. Maura went on to acquire a master's degree in anthropology and then was offered a position to teach at the university as well. Colleen married a stone mason and stayed in the Maryhill section of Glasgow.

"Hello, it's Maura...I told you I would call if I heard anything." Maura had shared her birth secret with Colleen when she first received Tim's letter. "No, it's not good news, but it wasn't the operation that killed Tim." She described the contents of Sister Calista's letter.

"What a terrible shame," her half-sister said, trying to console her. "But look at the bright side, you have a Yankee sister. She said she intends to visit after the holidays. That should be wonderful. You'll get to share time together, and you both are teachers so I'm sure there will be a great deal to talk about." She went on trying to cheer Maura for the longest time. Maura realized what she was trying to do, and it did in fact help her realize her other half-sister would soon be paying a visit.

"Thanks Colleen, I just couldn't face a room full of students today." They went on to talk about Colleen's husband, Carl, and their three children. Ever since Sheilah had died, Colleen had opened her home to Maura, and sometimes they shared the holidays. "Don't forget to ask the children what they want for Christmas, and drop me a line. I'm looking forward to seeing you and them."

Maura hung the phone up. She felt much better after talking to Colleen. Usually her Christmas and Easter holidays were spent in Paris with Claude DuBois. For the past five years, she and Claude, who was also a professor teaching classes on anthropology, had been having a secret affair. They started as friends when he first migrated from French Morocco. Both had represented the university on digs during their summer sabbaticals. It was during these encounters, working so closely together, that they had realized that they were in love with each other. Claude was single, but he knew his family would disown him if he ever married a white woman. Maura almost welcomed the obstacle, because as much as she loved him, she enjoyed her single life and the aura of secrecy surrounding the affair.

The rain had stopped about one o'clock, just after Maura returned from walking Abigail, her white-haired terrier. As she shook her umbrella and tried to unleash the dog, her phone rang.

"No, I'm fine," she answered.

"No, Claude, there's no need for you to come after your class. Really, I'm fine. It's just that the news from abroad shook me. I was hoping my brother and sister would survive the implant, but other things took over." She then went into the full details. "This will have some affect on our holiday plans this Christmas. My sister said she would like to visit at that time, so we'll have to postpone our trip." Maura had confided in Claude as well as Colleen about her sudden addition to her family. She kept him up to date with each of Tim's letters.

"I understand; are you certain you don't want me to stop by on my way home tonight?"

"Yes, I'll be all right. I spoke to Colleen this morning for a long time, and she helped me a great deal. I think I'll just relax, take a warm bath, take a few aspirins, and go to bed early. Did you happen to see the notice I asked the office to put in my classroom?"

"Yes, that's how I found out. When I went down to the office, they told me you had called in and mentioned bad news from abroad. I realized it had to do with the operation you told me about."

"I had scheduled a test for this morning; hopefully the students took the extra time to study."

"Could be. From some conversations I overheard, the students were glad for your unexpected absence. I certainly can't say the same. But I'll see you tomorrow. I love you."

"I love you too, Claude; see you tomorrow. Maura stoked the fire she had started earlier and placed another log on. As she stared into the fire, a thought grasped at her that brought her to fall into a nearby chair. Not once in any of his letters did he ask if she would come forward and volunteer a lung in the event his wasn't compatible for her sister. *Tim never made such a request*, she thought, *but I'm sure it was on his mind. Why else would he break a promise made to his mother?* In spite of the fact she was glad of her new-found family, she didn't feel that strongly about such a generous donation. Guilt about how she felt now that he was dead seized her being. The letters she had written to Tim were now being read by Sister Calista, and she wondered if her selfish attitude came through.

Chapter Nineteen

Maura went to bed early that night. She sat there re-reading all of Tim's letters. After Claude had called, she took a relaxing bath and fixed a light supper: a grilled cheese sandwich and soup.

The shock of Tim's death awakened the strongest emotion she first experienced at his first letter—*anger*. All those years she had wondered about her birth parents, and now to find out she had a family, a brother and sister… The realization that Sheilah knew and chose to keep the secret didn't sit too well either.

"How could someone just abandon a baby?" She remembered her conversation with Claude the day of the first letter.

"Don't be so quick to judge; from what you have told me your mother didn't have much choice. She couldn't very well tell her husband you were his child, could she? You were fortunate to have had Sheilah as a surrogate mother." He smiled.

"I know, but all those years fantasizing all kinds of scenarios, a single woman abandoned by her lover, no means of support for her and me. You will never know how many times I daydreamed about this."

"Well, consider your search at an end. Enjoy your new-found family," he said.

Maura fingered through the rest of the letters looking for the one that told of their early childhood in the Bronx; of cold winters sleighing in the lots next door to where they lived, the contingent of neighborhood children in the summer months running through the abandoned, broken structures. With her eyes closed, she imagined herself as a small child running along with the group. In another letter he told of how he had been drawn to the priesthood as a young man and his many years of study in the seminary. He wrote and told of Una's years in investment banking and how she decided to change careers and go into teaching and then finally the convent. These letters gave her a window into how her past might have been, and she envied a childhood that included other siblings.

She awoke early the next day, before the alarm went off. As she sat and sipped her coffee, a thought crossed her mind about the irony of Tim's death. *If he hadn't died, I wonder if he would have told my sister about me. All this discovery about our family hinged on his death and letters we had written to one another.*

She took the packet out of her robe pocket. These letters attached themselves to her person, like an umbilical cord tied to an infant at birth. They documented her roots. The last letter was dated in late September, and he told her the date of the operation and made mention of Sister preparing for the debate in November. He also wrote about the topic that was to be debated: Roe vs. Wade. She finished reading portions that made her smile. He certainly had a wonderful wit about him. It's a shame. The letters lay on the kitchen table while she cleared away her coffee cup. She looked up at the clock on the wall and started to move faster. *I better get a move on or I'll miss another day.*

"Maura, wait up." She recognized the familiar voice and turned to see his smiling face. "I saw you leave the bus and have been calling you."

She stood on the pavement returning the smile. "I'm sorry; I've been rushing. I wanted to get to class before any of my students. I have handouts to arrange for this test, and I didn't want to take too much time away from the students."

"How are you feeling? I'm so sorry about Tim. It certainly was strange about the circumstances surrounding his death."

"I was thinking the same thing myself this morning. I've been reading his letters and enjoyed his humor and sense of enjoyment of life. I'm glad that I have his letters; they're like travel cards back into the past when I want to know what my life could have been."

"That's a good way to look at it."

Students started to converge on the pair as they started up the stairs of the college. As they entered the doors, they said their goodbyes and went their separate ways.

After her second class of the day, she took the afternoon bus, stopping at the market to buy things necessary for the couple's usual Wednesday night supper. Even though there was no mention of dinner when the couple met at school, the date was a ritual for several years. Claude usually spent the night and left early in the morning. Maura looked forward to this particular dinner. She wanted to talk to him about the recent events. The suddenness of Tim's death awakened in her the realization of how fragile life is.

"Claude, I know this may seem silly to you, but ever since I received news of Tim's death I can't seem to get it out of my mind."

"Get what out of your mind?" He put down his coffee cup and gently grasped her hand.

"How quickly one's life can be snuffed out. Here my brother was, on his way to dinner after surviving a life-threatening operation that possibly could have taken his life, and for no other reason but money he is dead. I just can't comprehend it." She took the letters out of her pocket and laid them on the table.

"May I?" Claude asked as he picked up one of the letters.

"Go ahead; you will appreciate his way with words. That's one of the reasons I shall regret not having met him. I felt the exchange in our letters was an introduction into something much more about us."

"This one says upon her release from the hospital she has a national debate in Washington, D.C., to attend with some of her students. That should be interesting to watch; maybe our BBC will broadcast it. We sometimes catch telecasts of college debates. This one may, given the resolution—Resolved—Should Roe vs. Wade Be Overturned. It's to be held sometime in late November."

Claude's mention of the debate seemed to lift Maura out of her sadness. "Abortion, how in the world could the Supreme Court of the United States have passed such a liberal policy?" He intended to keep up the discussion in order to lift Maura's spirits.

"I'm glad we don't have such a policy." As an afterthought she added, "If we did, I might not even be here."

"You're right, and I'm very happy about that." He rose from his chair, and hugged her around the waist. "Very glad we have no such policy."

After the dishes were done, the couple retired to the living room. Claude kept up reinforcing Maura, trying to cheer her up.

"Look at your childhood with, Sheilah. She gave you all of her love and raised you like you were her very own daughter. Possibly, you never would have been afforded the music lessons and schooling had you been raised in America. These letters tell of children raised in not too much luxury. It may seem romantic of you to wish you could have been there too, but given the circumstances surrounding your birth, would your American father ever have accepted you? And as far as your real father, Mickey Bradey, from what you have told me about him, the only good thing he produced for you was your other half-sister Colleen."

"You're right, it's just that the news came as such a shock; I couldn't see the whole picture. Sheilah couldn't have done enough for me as a child growing up. She doted on my every whim. How could I ever say in all honesty I had an unhappy childhood? And you're right about my real father; after what Colleen has told me about his escapades, I've been fortunate to be spared his everyday presence. It's just that I felt a sense of guilt knowing that my sister is reading the letters and nowhere in them do I mention I would have offered my lung as a transplant in the event Tim's didn't match."

"Well, he never mentioned it to you."

"I know, but I'm sure it had been in the back of his mind. Why would he even start the correspondence after all these years of silence?"

"You're probably right, but it didn't work out that way, so why don't you let it go. From her letter she seems anxious to meet up with you, and that is what you should stay focused on right now and stop dwelling on the past. I suppose our trip to Paris at Christmas will be postponed if you're expecting a visit from your sister."

"She never mentioned the exact dates, but I imagine it will be the week between Christmas and New Year's. We could let it go until spring, but that seems such a long way off. I'll write to her this week and see if I can firm up the exact dates. I'll suggest a mid-week visit, say, Tuesday through Thursday, and in this way you and I could spend the weekend together."

"Perfect, my love," he kissed her passionately and she responded to the warmness of his body as his hand gently caressed the back of her head, and he pulled the lamp chord, leaving the room in darkness.

Chapter Twenty

Julia thought about asking Sister Calista for Thanksgiving dinner. Since receiving her note, she felt sorry for all the nun had been through. Clifford thought it would be a good idea as well, and when Bridget called one evening Julia mentioned it.

"I'm thinking of asking Sister Calista to Thanksgiving dinner."

"That's kind of you, Mom; I'm sure it will be sad for her, this being the first one without her brother, Tim. She and he were very close. I think it's a great idea. Shall I extend the invitation or shall you?"

"You can mention it if you wish, but I'll ask her personally. Do you have her phone number?"

"Yes, I do." Bridget gave her mother Sister's number. "The best time to call is early morning or after supper. She's on the go most of the day."

"I'll call her this evening and let you know what she says."

"Great, I'll wait to hear from you before I mention anything."

Sister had just sealed the envelope on Maura's letter when her telephone rang.

"Hello Sister Calista, this is Julia Clark. How are you?"

"I'm fine." Sister was startled upon hearing a voice out of the past, and she sat down on the edge of her bed fiddling with chord. "And how are you getting on? Bridget tells me you're making great strides toward a full recovery."

"Yes, as a matter of fact I'm looking forward to a wonderful Thanksgiving. That's the reason for my call. Clifford, Bridget, and I would love to have you for Thanksgiving and hope you would be our house guest for the weekend." The surprise invitation made Sister realize that her usual Thanksgiving with Tim would be no more. Sister hadn't given much thought on the holiday since she was so wrapped up in the debate planning.

"I've been so busy with the debate preparation. I've never thought much about the holiday."

"Please say you'll come," Julia sensed doubt in her reply. "I think it would be good for all of us to share the holiday. You can relax; the debate will be over. Clifford and I would love to have you." Julia sounded sincere in extending the invitation and the thought of being alone prompted her to accept.

"If you don't think it will be too much trouble, I'd love to come."

"Good, you can hitch a ride with Bridget. This way you won't even have to drive."

"Thank you. I'll look forward to seeing you." Sister wondered if they ever fixed the latch on their front gate as she placed the phone back in its cradle.

The bus started to load its passengers the morning of the debate. Several parents paced back and forth, circling the bus, looking for daughters leaving dorm quarters. Laughter came from inside the bus as the students settled into their seats. Sister Calista, roster in hand, checked the team names upon entering the bus. Finally, all had been accounted for and at 9:00 A.M., amidst chattering females and proud parents, the bus left the parking lot.

Georgetown had prepared a luncheon for the competing teams and the bus, upon arrival, left its passengers at the cafeteria entrance.

"I'm starved," Patricia turned to Bridget as the passengers headed toward the door. "Hope they have something good, like Fajitas." Bridget laughed.

"I'll settle for a salad; I'm too nervous to eat anything else. I hope my dad gets down here in time."

"I'm sure he will, and relax, you did a great rehearsal. I love your summation."

"Thanks,"

A young man held the door open as the girls passed through, and both girls turned to look over their shoulders and smiled at one another. The cafeteria was noisy, crowded with students and parents from various colleges milling about looking for placement. Sections of the enormous room had signs on tables identifying where each college was to sit. Finally, the girls found their table and sat down.

"Glad you found us," Sister Calista said.

"Patricia is hoping for Fajitas being served." Bridget smiled at the group.

"I don't think that's a strange request, given its popularity," Patricia groused.

"I'm sure there will be a great deal to choose from." Sister said. "I believe you two were the last to come, but I see some lost parents over there; I'll just go over and usher them here."

After lunch Sister found out where the team could freshen up and prepare for the evening debate. Parents were left to their own devices. The girls found the rooms assigned to them adequate and managed some flirting with the seniors who showed them the rooms. Sister Calista ignored the harmless banter among the students and smiled. She realized this harmless display relaxed the girls, some of whom showed signs of anxiety, Bridget being one of them.

"You will have time before dinner to spend on your own, but please be back by 5:00 so we may all eat dinner together."

"I'm going over my notes." Bridget turned to Patricia, who flopped on one of the twin beds.

"Not me, I think I'll check to see if some of the others want to wander around Georgetown. I kind of like that guy who showed us our room. Maybe I can run into him." She kicked off her shoes and headed for the bathroom. "Right after I take a shower."

Bridget called the hotel her dad said he would be in.

"Has a Mr. Clifford Clark checked in?"

"One moment please, I'll check." The clerk put her on hold. "Yes shall I ring his room?"

"Please…Hello dad. I'm so glad you made it. No, I've had lunch…I want to go over my notes one more time."

"I understand, honey, but try and relax. Maybe it would do you good to get out and just walk around a bit."

"I'm fine dad. Patricia is doing just that, but I can't concentrate on sightseeing right now. Dinner is going to be served at 5:00 here in the cafeteria and parents are welcome. By then I should be all set."

"I'll grab a quick sandwich and then visit with an old friend for awhile, and I'll catch up with you at dinner, okay?"

"Great, see you then."

Patricia, hair dryer in hand, unwrapped the towel from her head and placed it on the back of the chair. The noise from the dryer ended conversation between the two, girls and Bridget hoped it wouldn't take long before she had the room to herself. A knock came to the door, and several of the debating students pounced into the room. By this time Patricia had dressed and applied makeup, ready to take on the Georgetown seniors. Finally, after all peeked into the bathroom, did a house inspection, the group left and Bridget settled down to concentrate on her notes.

Clifford called on an old college friend, Hank Sullivan. He hadn't seen him in a few years, and with the afternoon all to himself decided to call on him. They had been college roommates, and upon graduation Hank headed to Washington. Whenever they had cause to visit in their respective home states, the two men took time out to do a visit.

"So you're down here to cheer your daughter on in her debating prowess?" Hank smiled as he handed his friend a drink he mixed at the bar in his office. Clifford thought the two could go to lunch, but Hank begged off. Instead, he asked Clifford to join him in his office and they could share and ordered-in lunch. "I'm involved in an investigation of the two woman lawyers who brought the Roe vs. Wade Supreme Court decision."

"You're putting me on. Is this newsworthy stuff yet?" Hank's involvement with the Justice Department sometimes gave Clifford a jump on a headline for his publication.

"No, just some right-to-life organizations came up with suspicious depositions taken at the time of the original hearings and have come to Washington to start an investigation."

"My daughter will be glad to hear that; she is debating on that very same issue tonight. I'm sure she could have used that information."

"I suppose she could have, but it would probably take a few years before the organization can gather all the information it needs to prove its case. Is she defending or opposing the Supreme Court's ruling?"

"She's opposing the decision."

"Good for her. That ruling was based on such weak arguments. I'd like to see the ruling reversed myself."

"Tune in tonight. It airs on Public TV at 9." The two men reminisced about old college days and enjoyed the time Hank allowed from his heavy work load.

"My best to Julia," Clifford had explained Julia's absence. "That's too bad she won't be at the debate, but at least she will see it on TV I'll be sure to watch. Who knows, Bridget may be a litigator in the Justice Department someday." They both laughed at the remark and Clifford took his leave.

Patricia and the rest of the students on the debating team had an enjoyable afternoon flirting and exchanging phone numbers with some of the Georgetown upper classmen.

As soon as the women exited from their assigned quarters, the young eager men swarmed around them like locusts offering their assistance as guides on campus. When Patricia returned to the room, she chattered away nonstop about every detail!

"You should have come Bridget; what a nice bunch of guys we met."

"Did you ace in on your upperclassmen?" Bridget asked, looking up from the desk where she sat.

"As a matter of fact I did. His name is Larry Lonegan. He's from Bangor, Maine."

"Any future plans?"

"Well," Patricia flopped on the bed and added dreamily, "he said he'd stop by the college on his way home for Thanksgiving."

"Now that you've honed in on your prey," Bridget said kidding, "Let's get ready for dinner. We don't want to be late."

"Did you ever get in touch with your dad?" Patricia shouted from the shower. The question went unanswered as she realized the noise from the water and the closed door made it impossible to carry on any conversation. She repeated it later while towel drying her hair in the room.

"Yes, he wanted to go to lunch, but I told him we already had it. He will be here for dinner, though. Now, what shall I wear?" She held up two outfits and decided on a gray skirt with a yellow blouse.

When Clifford returned to his hotel, he called Julia.

"Are you all set for your daughter's debut on public TV?" He jokingly said.

"I certainly am. In fact I have invited some of the neighbors in just to add to the festivities. Lilly, next door, has been marvelous. She has been here since early this morning helping me get some appetizers together. I really haven't done much of anything except supervise. I'm so excited. Have you seen Bridget yet?"

"No, but I have spoken to her. She called the hotel. I thought we could go to lunch, but she had already eaten. I'll see her for dinner. The college has arranged dinner for students and parents. Oh, by the way, I stopped in to see Hank and I was surprised at learning what the Justice Department is involved in. Would you believe depositions taken during Roe vs. Wade are suspect?"

"What do you mean 'suspect'?"

"People may have lied about the facts surrounding the woman involved in seeking the abortion."

"How did that come about?"

"Some right-to-life group uncovered it and brought the evidence to Washington."

"How will it affect the ruling?"

Hank said it would take a couple of years to sort out the facts, but I'm sure it will make an impact."

"I guess Bridget could have used that information as well. Oh, well with the efforts she has put into her presentation, she is more than prepared."

"You're right there; she even stayed in her room to bone up on last-minute details instead of taking a tour with Patricia and some of her teammates."

"I guess she will be relieved when this is all over. It must be exhausting for her. I'll be rooting for her tonight. When you see her at dinner give her all my love."

"Will do. Enjoy the debate, I'll call you when I get back to the hotel if it's not too late."

"I'll be waiting to hear from you, goodbye."

Bridget and Patricia arrived at the dining hall and saw Sister Calista approaching from down the hall. Both girls waited at the doorway, and then all three entered the room. The noise in and around them made it difficult to carry on a conversation in normal tones, and the women found themselves shouting at each other.

"The acoustics in this place could stand improvement," Patricia shouted.

"There's our table over there," Bridget pointed her body toward the area with Patricia and Sister in tow. Clifford Clark didn't see his daughter approaching. He was busy talking to one of the students.

"Dad," Bridget couldn't contain herself any longer "Dad," she shouted again, and this time he turned in her direction. He quickly got up and ran to her, and they hugged each other. Patricia and Sister scooted around the happy reunion and sat down at the designated table assigned for them. Father and daughter joined the group, smiling. Clifford then took notice of Sister Calista. He hadn't seen her since that day in the restaurant, and he recalled the incident as he silently looked at Bridget. *She looks so much like her birth mother*, he thought to himself. *It's a wonder Bridget hadn't commented on it before.* It seemed eerie when he looked at his daughter and noticed the combination of the gray skirt and the yellow blouse she had on. Sister Calista had also taken notice of the man to whom she met briefly and decided to entrust him with her child. It seemed so long ago.

"Well ladies," Sister knew Patricia would be observing this reunion and didn't want to clutter her mind with any unnecessary emotional baggage that would interfere with her focus on the evening's event. She stood up and tried to shout over the noise in the room. "We have prepared for this debate for many months. You have worked and researched the material with discipline, and I'm sure because of it we are guaranteed a good chance of winning. At the mention of the word 'winning', all present let out a rousing cheer!"

The seating arrangements at the table allowed Sister to watch Clifford interact with his daughter. She sat opposite of them and every so often caught Clifford glancing in her direction.

The meal didn't last that long. The students, anxious to get back to their rooms and freshen up before air time, gulped dinner. Some hardly touched the main course and had salads or sandwiches. Parents, most of them, retreated as soon as their daughters did. Clifford stayed behind purposely to talk to Sister.

"It's been a long time since that day in the restaurant," Clifford started the conversation.

"Yes and I can't thank you and your wife enough for the wonderful job you both did in raising my daughter."

"Whoever thought our paths would cross after these many years and you would get to see her as a grown woman."

"For years I pictured her in various different stages of her development and wondered how she looked, what interested her. The day she showed up at the college left me in a state of happiness you would never have believed.

I might add that from the moment of the discovery I had no intention of upsetting her life or yours. It just so happened we hit it off, and working so close with her preparing her for this debate was a dream come true for me. I'm sorry that your wife suffered as a result of the research on abortion."

"I'm afraid that's my fault as well. My wife never would have had that abortion if I didn't pressure her. For years it prayed on her mind, and when all that talk about it came home, it must have been just too much for her and caused the breakdown."

"Well, let's hope this debate will make some people think about the long-term effects this has on the woman."

"You might be interested to know what I found out this afternoon from a friend of mine." Clifford told her the story Hank had revealed to him.

"I'm so glad when I was pregnant that I never thought abortion was an option. I suffered disappointment from Bridget's birth father but, possibly because he never knew about the baby, the decision was mine and mine to handle."

"I can still picture you in that restaurant, and I must say I'm so glad you had the courage to have Bridget."

The workers in the cafeteria were clearing tables close by and prompted Clifford to look up and say, "Lots has happened to you and me between our only encounter of lunch and dinner."

Sister smiled and they both exited the cafeteria.

Chapter Twenty-one

"I don't see why we have to allow protestors at a college debate," Security officer Ted Robbs said. The debate was due to start in an hour, and Robbs wanted to voice his opinion to Vice Principal Lewis McMahon. When Robbs had received the request from both the organizations, he had forwarded it to administration with a notation that he vehemently objected to it. He felt the college didn't have the manpower to control any unruly mobs if things got ugly and out of hand.

"It's a free society," McMahon said to the security officer as he paced back and forth. " I feel as you do, but my hands are tied. Our president has ordered to let the protestors picket as long as it's done in orderly fashion."

"I've yet to see anything orderly about any demonstrations on abortion. Emotions are deep rooted in people's belief systems. I'm not looking forward to facing these demonstrators."

"You must be firm and on the alert when letting them into the auditorium, warning them to remain silent while the debate is in progress and anyone causing a disturbance will be removed."

"Easier said than done," Robbs retorted.

"I don't envy you your job, Robbs, but I'm sure everything will go smoothly."

"I hope you're right…we'll have to wait and see."

Julia had a big fire going by the time her first guests arrived. The temperature had dropped to sixty-eight degrees within an hour after five, and she knew a fire would be welcome by her neighbors who had walked the short distance to her house.

"Let me take your jacket," Julia said to Alice Porter. Alice headed directly toward the fireplace.

"The first fire of the fall season," she rubbed her hands together and sat as close to it as possible. Other neighbors arrived soon after, and Julia circled the group, offering canapés and wine.

"You're looking well," volunteered Harry Chapman as he reached toward the tray Julia offered him.

"Thanks, Harry, it's been a painful recovery, but thank God I feel like my old self again." Julia turned her attention toward the TV and worked her way over toward it, chatting and making small talk along the way. She turned in to the station just in time to hear the announcer giving the time limits each debater had and the amount of time for rebuttal. A silence came over the gathering as they sat down in the seats Julia had scattered around the room.

Backstage, makeup people from Public TV were applying cosmetics to the participants in the debate. "If I knew I was going to be made over, I wouldn't have spent so much time on my face," Patricia said to Bridget. "Hope they do a good job; who knows, I might be discovered."

"Discovered for what?" Bridget turned to her, much to the annoyance of the makeup artist who was trying to apply eye shadow to her upper lids. "I think I look fine," she said, pushing out of the chair that had held her captive for the makeover. "I'm not used to all this on my face; I look like a kewpie doll."

"Can't stop anyone for what they think," said the clinician, gathering up her makeup products. "I get paid to make you look good before the cameras."

Bridget, Patrica, and the other students were led down a hallway, then onto a stage with lecterns dividing it for the debate. Other debaters joined the group and soon the scene was set. The curtain was drawn and exposed an audience hidden under the glare of TV camera lights. Bridget felt herself squinting to adjust to the glare from the lights. A priest from Georgetown came unto the stage and announced the rules for the debate. The debaters eyed each other from behind their lecterns. There were five on each side for a total of ten. The invitation to the debate had been sent out to numerous colleges throughout the country, and a committee from Georgetown selected the two colleges who submitted, in their opinion, the best facts uncovered by each school. The College of New Rochelle and Harvard University were the two schools chosen.

On the Harvard team there were three females and two male students. The priest gave final instructions and the debate commenced.

"That was an interesting point Bridget made about fathers not having say in a baby carried to term," said Harry Chapman. Julia's face at first beamed with pride and then she remembered how Clifford prodded her to having an abortion. Whoever thought her own daughter would be extolling the evils of abortion and its long-time effects? Bridget's life was never in jeopardy because a young woman never entertained such thoughts.

Alice Porter chimed in with the compliment Harry paid Bridget.

"She certainly has command of the English language," said Alice, turning around to address Julia." And her comparisons of O'Keeffe's charcoal sketches to modern-day sonograms."

"She never shirked from anything she strongly believed in," said Julia, smiling at Alice's remark. The group in the living room stayed fixed on the TV and words flew fast and furious between the debating teams. No one realized the hour going by so quickly. In summation Bridget pointed out that the Supreme Court based its decision on the fact that the State of Texas could not prove when human life began.

"Robert Flowers, Texas assistant attorney, argued a fetus is a human being from conception and therefore has constitutional rights. Sarah Weddington, the attorney representing Roe, rebutted Flower's argument claiming her client did not advocate abortion. Her argument lay in the foundation that an individual has a constitutional right to terminate a pregnancy. Weddington did not address the question posed by Flowers: "Who is speaking for the children?" Bridget's voice gained urgency as she glanced up at the clock and realized her time was almost up.

As her eyes came away from the clock, she noticed Sister Calista in the wings and their eyes met. Without thinking she pushed aside her prepared statement and blurted out, "I will speak for those children. The opinion written by Justice Blackmum set limits on when a woman could end a pregnancy. Only in the first three months of pregnancy could a woman secure an abortion. How could a court arbitrarily decide human life starts in the fourth month? The opinion raises troubling questions."

The College of New Rochelle received the most points and was declared the winner. Their team took the Supreme Court's ruling, which was based on the fact that the State of Texas did not prove when life began, and said the Supreme Court's decision to allow states to interfere with second and third trimester abortions compromised the ruling. This did not sit with the pro-choice advocates in the audience, and some of the group became unruly, shouting out and chanting their views. Security men rushed to the scene and ushered them outside the auditorium.

Once outside the building the unruly protestors took up the signs they left upon entering. Security guards fanned through the mob, using bullhorns to aid in dispersing the crowd. Their presence only fuelled the shouts to become louder. Camera crews exiting the building tried to film the mob scene, which only seemed to infuriate the protestors more. Grasping hands ripped TV cameras off the shoulders of reporters.

Inside jubilant cries of victory dominated the scene. Sister congratulated the girls and admonished them to thank the opposition for their performance, and the losing team reluctantly shook hands. The college had prepared a celebration in Grayson Hall, all the debaters and their families were invited to attend. "Come on, Bridget, hurry up, I want to get to the party and find my Prince Charming."

"I'm coming. I'm looking for my jacket. I left it in the room where we had all that war paint plastered on us. You go on ahead; I want to see if I can find my dad."

Sister Calista headed for the exit along with all the others. Once outside the shouts and chants of the demonstrators drowned out any normal conversation between people. Security guards tried unsuccessfully to disperse the mob but to no avail. The people exiting were jostled among the protestors. Students who opposed the shoving and pushing retaliated, and before long the school had called in for outside help to quell the disturbance. By the time Bridget reached the thick glass she could see the contorted faces of the mob-picketing demonstrators pushing and shoving. *How will I ever find my father in this bedlam?* thought Bridget as she viewed the surreal angry mob. She grasped the handle of the door.

"Bridget, over here, over here." Sister Calista spotted her in the doorway and again shouted out as loud as she could, "Bridget over here, over here." The nun wormed her way out of the sea of demonstrators and finally the two met up with each other.

Then came a shout out of the crowd. "There she is!" The words did not have a face on it, only a loud explosion. A gun went off and the crowd divided in a split second. A woman waving a gun stood in the split chasm.

"Bitch, who do you Catholics think you are? This is America and my body is mine. Stop trying to shove your beliefs on us." The woman's eyes bulged frog-like out of their sockets. She aimed the gun while the two women cowered outside the glass door.

"Sister, what shall we do?" implored Bridget, barely audible.

"Stay calm. I'm going to try to reason with her. Get in back of me but move very slowly." Just as Bridget ducked behind Sister, there was another shot. The nun fell to her knees. Someone from the crowd tackled the woman from behind and knocked the gun out of her hand. Security guards quickly led the woman away and a circle of people gathered around Bridget and Sister.

"Oh what kind of world do we live in?" cried Bridget, cradling Sister in her arms.

"One that certainly needs paying attention to," whispered Sister.

"Shh, save your strength. Don't talk."

"All right, I won't, but would you do something for me? Would you call me Mother just this once?"

Bridget leaned over Sister Calista, and through a stream of tears she uttered "Mother."